Praise for the writing of author C.J. Carmichael

"*A Little Secret Between Friends* is a must read, full of romance, mystery and surprising revelations. Talented C.J. Carmichael has penned a wonderful book for you and all your friends. I am sure you will find a special place for it on your keeper shelf."
—*CataRomance*

"From its roller-coaster beginning to its calm, smooth ending, C.J. Carmichael's moving story highlights redefining life's priorities and rediscovering love."
—*Romantic Times BOOKclub* on *Small-Town Girl*

"Ms. Carmichael carefully stitches together the viewpoints of her richly drawn characters until a full-bodied patchwork quilt of their lives and love is created."
—*Romantic Times BOOKclub* on *The Fourth Child*

"Ms. Carmichael writes powerful storylines that touch every reader's heart, thanks to the emotional depth, rich characterizations, complex plots and appealing characters....You really can't go wrong when you read a book by C.J. Carmichael."
—Diana Tidlund, *Writers Unlimited*, on "Deal of a Lifetime"

C.J. Carmichael

A former chartered accountant turned fiction author, C.J. Carmichael has published twenty novels with Harlequin. Highlights include a RITA® Award nomination for her Harlequin Superromance novel, *The Fourth Child* (which was also a *Romantic Times BOOKclub* Top Pick); a romantic-suspense career achievement nomination from *Romantic Times BOOKclub*; and a nomination for her Harlequin Intrigue novel, *Same Place, Same Time*, as *Romantic Times BOOKclub's* Reviewers' Choice Best Harlequin Intrigue of 2000.

C.J. lives in Calgary, Alberta, with two teenage daughters, and a dog and a cat. Please visit her at www.cjcarmichael.com. Or send mail to the following Canadian address: #1754-246 Stewart Green S.W., Calgary, Alberta, T3H 3C8, Canada.

HER BETTER HALF

C.J. Carmichael

HER BETTER HALF

Copyright © 2006 by Carla Daum

isbn-13: 978-0-373-88109-3

isbn-10:   0-373-88109-6

This edition published by arrangement with Harlequin Books S.A.

® and TM are trademarks of the publisher. Trademarks indicated with
® are registered in the United States Patent and Trademark Office, the
Canadian Trade Marks Office and in other countries.

TheNextNovel.com

PRINTED IN U.S.A.

Dear Reader,

While reading this book I'd like to ask you to think kindly
of the semidetached, World War I-vintage, run-down,
insulbrick-covered home that the heroine of this book,
Lauren, shares with her next-door neighbor Erin.

Think kindly of this house, because it is modeled exactly
on the first house my husband and I bought after we were
married. We were living in Toronto (as are the characters
in this book) and our house was on Thelma Avenue. It
was the worst house in a good neighborhood. It was the
worst house by quite a large margin. I still have nightmares
about the basement.

But I have only good memories about the porch, where
our daughter Lorelle practiced walking and climbing steps.
I have good memories of the claw-footed tub we painted
peach (it was the rage at the time). And I have good
memories of the dining room where we enjoyed many
happy meals with family and friends.

I hope you enjoy this story. I've been living with these
characters for years...it's hard to believe their story is
finally on paper.

Sincerely,

C.J. Carmichael

This book is dedicated to my daughter Lorelle,
as she takes her next big step
in life to leave home and go to university.
To paraphrase Lyle Lovett, follow your heart, Lorelle—
follow it with both your feet.

Big thanks to my former agent Linda Kruger, who
thought this book would make a good fit with NEXT.
More big thanks for help with various research questions
to Linda Prenioslo, Phil Daum and fellow Calgary
RWA members Julie Rowe and Florence Cardinal.

PROLOGUE

Rosedale, Toronto

On the day my husband left me, we were in the middle of a wicked heat wave in Toronto. Inside the bedroom of our estate home, air-conditioning masked the high temperatures and humidity. I actually felt cool as I watched Gary stuff a select few of his belongings into a backpack.

I noticed that his pants were loose around his waist. He'd dropped a few pounds since he'd adopted the vegetarian diet.

That had been six months ago. It had not been my first clue that my life was going to take a dramatic and unexpected turn. There'd actually been many, but I hadn't seen them at first. Or maybe I'd seen them but just refused to accept them for what they were: evidence that my husband was growing apart from me.

"I still think we ought to try counseling." I was proud of how calm I sounded. I would not be one of those shrieking women who went crazy and broke things and swore they'd kill themselves, or him, if he didn't stay.

"Counseling won't change anything. This has been a long time coming."

Too bad no one had told me.

But maybe I was letting myself off the hook too easily. I'd been the one to sign Gary up for the meditation course last winter. I'd seen his simmering anger, his mounting stress.

He'd been a man at the breaking point.

Until he'd found yoga. Or was it the yoga instructor? I still wasn't sure.

"Losing my job was the best thing that could have happened to me." He went to his sock drawer and picked through it, leaving all the fine wool dress socks behind. "It was a sign that I'm finally on the path to healing."

Oh, for Pete's sake! I was so sick of hearing about the "path to healing." This path didn't feel anything like healing to me. It felt like betrayal, and hurt and abandonment.

"Getting fired wasn't a sign, Gary." Who in their right mind considered losing a job a green light to desert your wife and children to go backpacking around the globe?

"How would you know, Lauren? Not to be cruel, but you're not exactly in tune with your spiritual side."

Despite the air-conditioning, my internal temperature jumped up a few degrees. "Oh, really?"

"You've never understood. Yoga isn't about postures, or fitness, or even relaxing. It's about spiritual growth. About achieving clarity and— Forget it. I can see you're not listening."

"I *am* listening. It's just that I don't happen to agree. Why can't you study yoga and achieve enlightenment here in Canada?"

It was time for my trump card. "What about the twins?"

But even that argument didn't move him.

"Jamie and Devin are almost grown up."

"They're *fourteen*."

"Well, they've always been closer to you, anyway. They'll be fine. They're good kids."

"Yes. Good kids who deserve more from their father."

"What do you want me to do? Go out and get

another job with another investment bank? Return to working twelve-hour days and six-day weeks? End up croaking from a heart attack at fifty like my old man?"

I couldn't stand the way he was talking to me. Like *he* was the intelligent, rational adult while I was the mental equivalent of a temperamental toddler. He was treating me and our marriage like an encumbrance to be gotten rid of in the same way as a bothersome outstanding balance on a mortgage.

"Don't you love me anymore?"

The question just came out. I hadn't planned to ask it. As I stood there waiting for his answer, I found myself remembering the girls when they were little, scrambling out of the pool after a swimming lesson, wet and shivering, waiting for me to wrap them in a towel.

Now I was the vulnerable one, waiting for Gary to throw me something. If not a towel, then maybe a facecloth.

"Lauren." He sighed. "I'll always love you. But things are different now."

I summoned my courage. "Is Melanie going on your backpacking trip, too?"

His mouth tightened. "This has nothing to do with Melanie."

"So she's not going?"

He didn't say anything.

Damn him. The bastard.

"I have an appointment booked with my lawyer this afternoon," I said. "Where should I have him send the papers?"

He straightened slowly. "You mean divorce papers?"

The D-word hung in the air between us. I couldn't believe I'd found the courage to deliver the ultimatum.

Please, please, please, I found myself praying to an unknown, unimagined entity. *Let Gary realize what I mean to him. What our family means to him.*

But he nodded, as if a divorce had been in his plans all along. Rather than trying to talk me out of legal action, he grabbed paper and pen and wrote down an address.

Melanie's no doubt.

Gary added one more pair of socks to the pack, then closed the flap.

"That's it? That's all you're taking?"

"You can sell the rest," he said, as if all the belongings he'd amassed over the past twenty years—the gold cufflinks, the Cartier watch, the twenty Harry Rosen suits lined up on his side of the closet—meant nothing to him.

I sank onto the bed. In stunned silence, I let Gary

kiss me on the forehead. I watched him sling the backpack over his shoulder, then walk out of our bedroom without a final glance.

"Don't forget to write." Ha-ha.

I collapsed onto the down comforter and wondered how I was going to tell the girls when they came home from camp.

CHAPTER 1

Dovercourt Village, Toronto
One year later

I stood back from the moving truck and took a long look at my half of the semidetached house that would be our new home. If it had any redeeming features, I couldn't see them. The place was old. Tired. Though I'd had the structure inspected and been assured of a dry basement and sound roof, the house looked as if a strong gale would send it toppling. Even the lawn and few scraggly shrubs appeared in need of resuscitation.

How was I going to make this place a home, a welcome sanctuary from the world for my girls and me?

The task seemed impossible.

I felt lost. Ever since Gary had left, I'd been losing

little bits of myself. They disappeared along with the people who had once constituted my world: my husband, our mutual friends, my in-laws and even my own parents. None of my relationships had emerged from this divorce intact.

And now my home was gone, too.

I sighed as I pulled out the envelope of cash for the mover. He accepted payment, handed me a receipt, then took off.

I wished I could do the same.

Toronto was a city of neighborhoods. Where you lived said a lot about you. My previous home in Rosedale had announced that I was part of the Toronto establishment—wealthy, privileged and entitled to the best the city had to offer.

This house, in this neighborhood, said blue-collar worker, unconnected, struggling to get by.

Those were hardly labels to aspire to. But a place in Dovercourt Village had been all I could afford within a reasonable distance of my daughters' private school.

Unfortunately, Gary and I had never been savers. We'd piled all his salary into our house and our extravagant lifestyle.

So here I was. Or, more accurately, here *we* were.

The new family unit—me, Devin, Jamie…that was it. Just the three of us now.

I brushed dust from my hands and headed for the front door. It was original to the house, too, protected by an ugly screen door. I'd have loved to rip the screen off, but maybe we'd need the extra insulation when winter came.

Inside, the foyer was so small it could hold no more than a couple people at the same time. With just two steps, I reached the stairs that led to the second story. I was heading for my bedroom, when I heard the doorbell.

Had the mover forgotten something?

I retraced my steps and opened the door. An attractive, but hard-looking young woman and a little girl stood on the front porch.

"Hi, I'm Erin Karmeli and this is my kid, Shelley. Welcome to the neighborhood." She slapped the wall that divided our two houses. "I'm your new neighbor."

I supplied her with my name and a smile that, despite my best efforts, must have looked hesitant.

Six months later, I would look back on this moment, on this first impression, and see Erin in a completely different light. Right now, though, I took in only a tall, thin woman with an improbably large bust displayed to advantage in a bright red tank top. Erin had striking, angular features, and wild, curly dark hair. Add in the miniskirt and high heels and there was no disputing what she looked like.

Just my luck. I've moved next door to a prostitute.

But there was the child to consider, a little girl about six years old, holding Erin's hand and gazing curiously down the hall at the stacked cardboard boxes. The girl had neat blond hair, wore clean denim overalls, and smelled—when I crouched to say hello—of toothpaste and sunscreen.

My mothering instincts approved on all counts.

"Are you in grade one, Shelley?"

She nodded, then said, "We made cookies."

Erin brushed a hand over the little girl's shoulder. "That's right. We did. We thought you might like to take a break and come for some iced tea on our porch."

She watched as I brushed my bangs from my forehead. My fingers came away tacky with sweat. No air-conditioning in this house.

Erin looked sympathetic. "Moving days are a bitch, aren't they?"

"Yes. They really are. And I'd love a break. Thanks, that's very hospitable of you."

"So you'll come?" Erin had a broad smile, not

without charm, despite crowded front teeth. "Great. Your kids are welcome, too."

"Actually, I'm pretty sure they're busy." Devin was organizing CDs in her new room, and Jamie was on the phone with an old friend.

Two years ago they would have dropped whatever they were doing to come with me. They'd still been girls then, not adolescents transformed—by what? Peer pressure and hormones?—into strangers.

I was reeling from more than just the divorce this year. My entire family had undergone a metamorphosis and I'd been too busy folding laundry to notice.

I felt like Sleeping Beauty. Only I'd fallen asleep in a castle and woken up in attached housing on the wrong side of the tracks next door to a...

Maybe Erin was a *drug addict*. She was *awfully* thin.

"I'll just be a minute while I tell the girls where I'm going." I paused, wondering if I should invite Erin and her daughter in to wait. But Erin solved my dilemma.

"We'll go home and get things organized. Meet us on the front porch?"

"Okay."

I headed upstairs, thinking that at least I'd been able to afford a place where the girls didn't need to share a room. It would be bad enough having them fight over the bathroom. In Rosedale, they'd each had their own, as well as a walk-in closet. I tapped on the first closed door, then opened it.

Boxes were piled everywhere—only a few had been opened. Jamie, dark hair twisted on her head, wearing baggy pajama bottoms and a tight, short tank top, sat in the middle of her bare mattress, talking on her cell phone. Jamie was always on that phone—she was going to have a fit when I had it disconnected. According to my new budget, I couldn't afford it.

"Jamie? I'm going next door to the neighbor's."

"Yeah, whatever, Mom."

"Also, could you please get off the cell phone. The landline is free, remember."

Jamie rolled her vivid blue eyes, outlined in dark liner and mascara.

Devin, in the next room, was crouched on the floor stacking her CDs in alphabetical piles. She was a quieter girl, more of a pleaser, a little more introverted. It was amazing to me that birth order could matter when you had twins, but in my daughters' case it really had. Devin had been born only two minutes after her sister, yet she seemed fated to forever be just so slightly in Jamie's shadow.

"I've been invited to the neighbor's for iced tea. Would you like to come, too? She has a little daughter—could be some babysitting jobs in your future."

"I'd like to finish this, Mom. Then I need to make lesson plans for next week."

Instead of sending the girls to their summer camp in the Muskokas this year—they would have been junior counselors—I had suggested they teach swimming at the country club where Gary and I had once been members. That way they could earn pocket money for the upcoming school year. I was proud of them for not complaining too much about the arrangement. Basically, it seemed Gary had been right.

The girls were okay. They were dealing with the divorce and all the changes to their lives better than I could have hoped.

I closed Devin's door gently, then headed to Erin's by myself.

Outside, I took stock of my new neighborhood. Just three months ago my real-estate agent had called with the news. "I've found a place within the budget. It's on Carbon Road, in Dovercourt Village."

What a quaint name, I'd thought, *Dovercourt Village*.

Of course many things, in theory, were quaint.

Wheelbarrows, country roads, watering cans, to name a few. In reality though, wheelbarrows were used to haul dirt and country roads were dusty in hot weather and impassable after rain. As for watering cans, well fine. Maybe they truly did qualify as quaint.

But Carbon Road was just an L-shaped street lined with World War I vintage homes in pairs like mine and Erin's.

A short hedge, about two feet high, separated our properties, and after a brief hesitation, I decided to step over it rather than walk around.

Erin and Shelley were sitting out on the white porch. Shelley waved shyly. Heavens but she was cute with her chubby cheeks and baby-toothed smile. I remembered my daughters at that age. The three of us had had so much fun together. Trips to the zoo and the playground, baking cookies, reading books at night.

When did kids stop wanting to do those things?

I stopped at the bottom of the porch steps. A small wicker table held a pitcher of iced tea and a stack of plastic glasses. On one of the steps, exposed to the hot summer sun, perched a clay pot of snapdragons.

Why did I feel reluctant to go farther? Erin was so different from the kind of neighbors I'd been used to. So different from me. Despite the fact that I probably had about fifteen years on her, I was sure she was far more experienced in the ways of the world.

I felt, as ridiculous as it sounds to say it—shy.

Erin waved me closer. "Grab a chair and relax. It's too hot to unpack boxes today, anyway."

"True." I pushed myself forward, and was surprised to find the wicker chair more comfortable than it looked. I took a deep breath. *This is supposed to be fun, Lauren.* "Thanks again for inviting me."

"Hey, we're going to be neighbors. We might as well get to know each other."

Erin lapsed into silence, apparently in no hurry on the getting-to-know-one-another plan.

Shaded from the sun, relaxing in the chair, sipping the cold tea…I finally felt myself loosen up. Looking over the scene before me, my attention was caught by a big black shape in the front window. "You have a piano. Do you play?"

"Mommy *teaches* the piano," Shelley said, crumbs clinging to the baby down on her cheeks.

"*Really?*"

"My students generally come in the evenings, some after school, others after dinner. I hope the noise won't bother you too much."

A *piano teacher!* The instant relief I felt cooled me

more than any beverage ever could. My next-door neighbor was a piano teacher. That would teach me to judge people based on appearances.

"Mommy works at night, too," Shelley volunteered. "Sometimes all night long. It's dodgy and I haffta stay with Lacey or sometimes Murphy."

Oh no. Alarmed and embarrassed, I wasn't sure where to look. To my surprise, though, Erin just laughed.

"Who told you Mommy's work was dodgy?"

"Lacey did. She says one day the police are going to come knocking at our door."

"That old busybody." Erin brushed crumbs from her daughter's overalls. "My work isn't dodgy. Lacey only wishes it was."

"Why does she wish it was, Mommy?"

"'Cause she's bored and lonely and needs something to think about."

"Lacey isn't lonely. She has lots of cats."

"Exactly." Erin turned to me. "Have you met our lovely Lacey yet? She likes to bring cookies over to new neighbors so she can check them out."

"She came by about five minutes after we arrived with the moving truck," I admitted. A short, ditzy-looking woman with frizzy hair and round glasses that had reminded the girls of Harry Potter.

"She lives across the street." Erin pointed at the yellow house directly opposite us. "The place has a cat door. Animals run in and out all the time. Whenever she spends the night, Shelley comes home covered in cat hair. Fortunately she doesn't have allergies. At least, not yet. Do your daughters babysit?"

Though I'd anticipated this question earlier, now I felt taken off guard. Shelley was a sweet little girl, but I wasn't sure I wanted the twins to babysit for Erin until I knew more about her home situation.

"Are they twins? How old are they?" Erin asked.

Trapped, I answered, "Fifteen."

This was all Gary's fault. If he hadn't deserted us, I wouldn't be in this situation, trying to find a polite excuse for not allowing our daughters to babysit so that this woman could—

What? Have sex for money? Sell drugs in dark alleys?

"Well, if they're interested in babysitting, I could sure use a backup for Lacey. I own my own business," Erin finally explained. "Creative Investigations."

"Is it…do you mean you're a private investigator?"

Erin nodded and my interest was piqued. I'd loved mystery novels since I'd devoured volumes of Encyclopedia Brown as a kid.

But books were one thing. Real life investigations were undoubtedly something different. "That sounds like it could be slightly…" I checked to see if Shelley was listening, but the little girl had moved to the far end of the porch and was playing with LEGO. I lowered my voice to a whisper. "…dangerous?"

Erin laughed. "Not at all. I *never* take on anything with the potential to get, you know, *messy*."

"The late-night assignments Shelley mentioned…?"

"Stakeouts. Sounds exciting, but trust me, they're not. Mostly I'm just out to catch cheaters. Adultery. Insurance fraud. You know, dull stuff like that."

Dull stuff?

"Hey, do you have the time?"

I checked the gold bracelet on my arm. "Almost one."

"Good." She pulled a bottle of vodka out from under her chair. "What do you say, Lauren?"

Vodka before dinner on a Tuesday afternoon?

I couldn't make up my mind about Erin Karmeli. One minute she seemed okay, just another mother, like me. The piano teaching was certainly respectable enough. But Erin was also a private investigator, who looked like a hooker and might possibly be an alcoholic as well as a drug addict.

On the other hand…like it or not, this woman was now my closest neighbor. And this was my new life. And when in Rome…

"Sure." I held up my glass. "I wouldn't mind a little."

CHAPTER 2

In high school I had known girls like Erin. They hadn't been my friends, but I'd seen them in the hallways— usually tucked under the arm of a hot football player. In class those girls sat at the back of the room, painting their nails and passing notes—usually to the hot football player sitting next to them.

Though these back-of-the-room girls seemed steeped in self-confidence and sophistication, I—with my high grades, tidy bedroom and a best friend I'd had since kindergarten—had somehow felt superior to them.

At sixteen, I'd thought I had life all figured out. Life rewarded those who made smart choices. Smart choices included obtaining a post-secondary education, marrying a hardworking, responsible man, making a beautiful home, and raising children.

Follow the rules and you'll be happy.

For more than forty years that philosophy had worked for me. Or so I'd thought.

Maybe the girls at the back of the class had had the right idea all along.

I gulped my first glass of tea and vodka like it was water. The warmth of the afternoon sun seeped through my clothing and skin, right into my bones, and it felt good. I sank lower in my chair, deliberately not thinking about the boxes waiting to be unpacked, the beds to be made, the cupboards to be washed out and restocked with staples from flour to vanilla extract. *Artificial* extract, now.

Erin mixed me another drink.

"So, Lauren, what's your deal? You don't wear a wedding ring. You divorced?"

It was an obvious question, one I should have expected, yet I could feel my defenses rising. I hated telling people I was divorced. It made me feel like such a loser.

After Gary had left me, I'd found myself observing women my age, married women with wedding bands on their fingers. I'd seen them in the shops, on the street, at the girls' school.

What had these women done right that I'd done

wrong? Why did their husbands still love them? Wasn't I good enough, smart enough, pretty enough?

The fact that my mother kept asking me these questions, too, hadn't helped.

"My husband left me about a year ago. He's in India now."

"India? Why the hell did he go to India?"

People didn't usually ask me that question. At this point they were usually searching for a new topic of conversation.

But Erin had open curiosity in her eyes. And the next thing I knew, I was saying something completely outrageous.

The truth.

"It all started with the meditation courses. Gary seemed so stressed, I signed him up for a program at our local community center."

"The sitting cross-legged on the floor and humming sort of meditation?"

"Yes. I thought he needed to learn how to relax."

"I take it he learned?"

"Oh, yeah. Next thing I knew he was signed up for Karma yoga. He'd go straight from work to the yoga studio."

"A real convert."

"Yes. He became another person, with a whole different set of values. Gary started talking about approaching every task with the right motive and doing your best and giving up on the results."

"Sounds cool."

"Well, his bosses didn't think it was so cool. They were actually pretty fixated on results, and when Gary stopped producing them, he was fired."

"Wow. And I thought yoga was just something you did for exercise."

"No, no, no." I waved my free hand in the air, the one that wasn't holding my drink. My head felt a little spinny and my tongue a little thicker, but these weren't bad feelings.

In a way, spilling this stuff out to a virtual stranger felt good. I hadn't been able to confide in any of my old friends or neighbors about this madness. I'd been too mortified.

But Erin was different. There was no judgment in her eyes, no condemnation—and most importantly of all—no pity.

"For Gary the yoga became a life-altering experience. He changed his diet, his wardrobe, even his manner of speaking. Really, he became a totally different person."

"Sounds like a born-again Christian."

"That's what it was like, exactly. Whenever I'd complain, Gary would tell me that yoga is all about reaching a state of consciousness that allows you to achieve union with the divine."

Erin nodded knowingly. "Or at least union with the hot little yoga instructor."

I stared at her mutely. How had she guessed?

Answering my unspoken question, Erin said simply, "Men."

"Gary didn't want to admit that he was leaving me for another woman. He preferred to pretend that he was seeking spiritual revitalization."

"What a bunch of crap."

"Exactly. How can lying to your kids and cheating on your wife make you a better person?"

"Only a man could make that logic work," Erin agreed. "So what finally happened? Did you tell him you'd had enough and kick him out the door?"

If only. At least then I might have retained some shred of pride and dignity. But I'd figured yoga would turn out to be another phase, like Gary's mountain-climbing stage. When the girls were little, he'd decided he wanted to climb the seven highest peaks in the world. He'd started with a non-technical climb to see how he would react to high altitudes. After he returned home from Mount Aconcagua in Argentina, he'd never mentioned mountain climbing again.

I had expected the yoga to follow the same pattern.

"I didn't have to ask. Gary left *me*. He said he needed space. To travel and be free."

"Let me guess…his freedom included the yoga babe?"

There was no need to answer what we both knew was a rhetorical question. I lifted my hair off the back of my neck. The heat was getting to me. Or maybe it was the alcohol. How many drinks had I had now?

"So, like, what's the situation?" Erin asked. "Your husband's gone. But he left you with money, right? You and the girls are taken care of?"

If I had money, would I have moved into this neighborhood?

The proceeds from selling our house were financing Gary's travels and this new house on Carbon Road. Our retirement funds and small investment account were earmarked for the girls' education, not everyday living expenses.

My shoulders slumped. What was the point in pretending anymore? "The situation is kind of depressing, to tell you the truth. I need to get a job. And quick."

"Have you got qualifications?"

"A history major."

Erin shook her head. "I meant something that would help you get a job."

I covered my face with my hands. "No. None of those kind of qualifications." God help me, I was a throwback to the fifties. A stay-at-home mom with no relevance to the real world.

I set my glass on the table and Erin refilled it, only this time she didn't add any vodka.

"You're screwed, girl."

"I know it." I was going to have to get a job working in a grocery store. Or maybe in a factory. I could just see myself, a week from now, toiling for minimum wage in a sweatshop in a basement on Queen Street where I'd be harassed by the middle-aged, overweight male boss for sexual favors....

I tried to stand and that was when I realized just how much I'd had to drink. Great. Now I was going to cap off one of the worst days of my life by passing out on my new neighbor's porch.

And to think I'd been the one judging Erin Karmeli when I'd first met her.

"I don't usually drink in the afternoon," I tried to say, not sure how the words actually came out sounding.

"Yeah, you wait until the kids are in bed, right?"

"No!"

Erin laughed. "Relax. I know you're a straight arrow. Believe me, I can always spot the other kind. Why don't you sit until the dizziness passes?"

"You probably have things to do...." I demurred. But still, I sat. I didn't really have any other option.

"Nothing pressing. Besides, I think I have just the solution for you."

"Oh?" I pretended interest. Everyone close to me had given their own well-meaning advice. My mother wanted the girls and me to move back home. My friends thought I should have a wild affair, then sue Gary for child support and force him to come home and get a job. My kids wished I could wave a magic wand and somehow get their father back, along with the house and everything else.

"You need a job, right? As it happens, I have so much business right now, I've been turning away clients. How would you like to work as a private investigator?"

A *private investigator*. Some long-buried sense of adventure burned inside of me at those words.

A private investigator.

I thought of the Sue Grafton mystery series I liked so

much. I wouldn't be Lauren Anderson Holloway, *dull mother and divorcée*, anymore. I would be like Kinsey Millhone...an edgy, exciting, interesting private investigator.

Wait a minute. Who was I kidding? Kinsey Millhone didn't cook and do laundry and organize appointments for her family. She ran on the beach, talked tough and knew how to use a gun.

I couldn't be a private eye. I wasn't brave enough for starters. I had no investigative skills.

"I can't, Erin."

"Why not?"

"I don't know how."

"Neither did I, until I started. I learned on the job...just like you're going to."

"But—" It had to be more complicated than that. "Wouldn't I need to be licensed?"

"Sure. You have a record?"

It took me a moment to realize she was referring to a *criminal* record. "No."

"Then it's a snap. We fill in the forms and write the check. We can do it tomorrow!" Erin narrowed her eyes. "That's if you want the job. I don't want to pressure you."

Maybe Erin didn't want to pressure me, but my

bank manager soon would. What were my options? What did I really have to lose?

"I'll take the job."

I could at least give it a try.

A week later, I was on Dupont Street, searching for the diner where I was supposed to meet Erin for lunch. Erin was planning to brief me on our first surveillance job. It was happening tonight, after dark. Though I would be with Erin, my stomach tightened and gurgled at the very thought of spying on another person.

As Erin had promised, it hadn't been difficult for me to get my license to operate as a private investigator. And yesterday Erin had helped me sign up for an online course that would teach me the basics of the job. It was all happening quickly and I had the sense that I couldn't stop it if I tried.

Not that I wanted to. I'd signed an agreement with Erin and the money was way better than I could have hoped for.

On the other side of the road, I spotted the place Erin had told me about. Murphy's Grill was wedged between a hardware store and a tattoo parlor on the sunny side of Dupont Street. The signage was old and missing one *l*. The building itself was red brick with a line of rectangular windows facing out to the street. Everything…the sign, the bricks, the glass…looked tired and just a little grimy.

Why did Erin want to meet here?

I crossed on a green light and passed the owner-operated hardware store where I'd gone to purchase cleaning supplies a few days ago. Denny Stavinsky had been keen to offer advice on everything from furnace filters to bathroom caulking. In so doing, he'd managed to slip in the fact that his wife had died seven years ago and that his son, his ungrateful son, only visited once a year around Christmas.

This neighborhood is my life, Denny had told me. *The people here are the best. I'm sure you and your daughters will be very happy here.*

I stopped at the diner door and glanced farther down the street. Past the tattoo parlor was a pawnshop, then a consignment clothing store. Garbage for tomorrow's pickup was already lined along the curb. Rosedale, this was not.

Welcome to my neighborhood.

I sighed, then leaned my shoulder into the door. The first thing I noticed was the smell. A fast-food combination of coffee and French fries and grilled meat. Facing me was a long counter lined with stools.

Behind the counter stood a broad-shouldered guy in a plaid shirt. He looked more like a lumberjack than someone working in the food services industry.

Was this Murphy? He met my gaze for a moment and I had the odd sense that he somehow disapproved of me.

I surveyed the long, narrow room, disappointed to see there were no booths or tables, just another counter along the window with more stools.

Perhaps Murphy didn't want to encourage the sort of customers who lingered over their meals.

Or perhaps his weren't the sort of meals one ever wished to linger over.

I settled on one of the stools facing the kitchen and surreptitiously studied the lumberjack. He had strong features, dark coloring, a grim set to his mouth. In high school he would have been one of the kids in the last row, handing notes back and forth to the girls like Erin.

I had always wondered what happened to bad boys after high school. I should have guessed they opened greasy spoons in suspect neighborhoods.

Something in this diner had to be good, though, because most of the stools were occupied, primarily by men. They were of all ages, most dressed in workmen's clothing, heavy boots, grimy T-shirts.

I glanced back at the big, broad-shouldered guy behind the counter. He hadn't shaved in about two days. His hair was on the long side, but it had been brushed, and his hands looked clean, too, I was relieved to note when he slid a coffee cup in front of me. He proceeded to fill it without even asking if I wanted any.

"You're Erin's new neighbor, I take it?"

"How did you know?"

"Just a lucky guess. I don't get many customers who wear pearls."

I put a hand to my throat. Gary had given me the necklace for our ten-year anniversary. For some reason I hadn't been able to take it off since I'd signed the divorce papers. I'd removed my rings, storing them in the deposit box at the bank for the girls when they were older.

But the pearls I hadn't been able to part with. They were the last link to my past, to the person I'd been.

"You okay?"

Murphy was looking at me as if he found me strange. Gathering my composure, I held out my hand. "Lauren Holloway."

"Murphy Jones."

His grip felt overwhelming, calloused, warm.

"Welcome to the neighborhood."

Was that a smirk at the corner of his mouth? It came and went so quickly, I couldn't tell for sure. "Thanks." I cleared my throat. "This is a nice place. Have you been open here long?"

"A nice place, huh? I'm glad you think so." Murphy tossed me a menu. "Take a look and give me a shout when you know what you want."

I watched him head for the kitchen, noting narrow hips and long legs. An order pad and a pencil peeked out the back pocket of his jeans.

I glanced around again, and several of the other customers quickly averted their heads. No doubt I stood out from the usual Murphy's Grill patron in my skirt and heels. Perhaps I should have gone for a more casual look.

Bells above the door jangled and Erin entered. Now *she* was dressed exactly right for this place, in a tight faded jean skirt and several layered tank tops. Her left wrist was covered in silver bangles and her dark hair curled madly in the late summer humidity.

"You found it okay?"

"Hard to miss." I moved my purse and Erin scooted onto the stool next to me. The guy on the next stool over took great interest in Erin crossing her legs.

"And was I right about the coffee? Better than Star-bucks, huh?"

"Twice as strong and half the price," Murphy said, appearing in time to fill Erin's travel mug just as she finished unscrewing the lid. "You gals want steak sandwiches?"

"Have you got anything better to offer?" Erin asked.

"What do you think?"

"I'll have a steak sandwich. Have you met Lauren?"

"We've met. What do you say, Lauren? Steak sandwich?"

I wondered about the relationship between these two. There was a tension in their body language that belied the nonchalance of the conversation. I opened the menu and scanned the lunch selections. "How about a BLT?"

He shrugged. "If you say so."

As soon as he'd moved on to give our orders to the kitchen, Erin squeezed my arm. "So? Are you excited?"

My stomach started up with the gyrations again.

"Your first stakeout." Erin sounded like a proud mother. "I remember my first time. It was kind of a letdown to tell you the truth."

"Must have been with the wrong guy," Murphy said, returning to his position behind the counter.

"Oh shut up and cook eggs or something. For your information we weren't talking about sex."

The guy next to Erin was openly staring now. Erin turned her back to him.

"Um." I leaned in close to her so I wouldn't be overheard. "What is our assignment, exactly?" Erin had been very sketchy with details up to this point.

"It's a simple adultery case."

Oh, really? Simple adultery. As compared to what…complicated adultery? I wondered if I would ever take this work as cavalierly as Erin appeared to.

I took another sip of my coffee and it was all I could do not to make a face. It was so bitter and sharp compared to the lattes I preferred. How did Erin drink such quantities of this stuff? Still, I supposed I'd better get used to it. On my budget I could no longer afford Starbucks. "So what do I do?"

Erin removed an envelope from the canvas pack she'd been carrying. "Sherry Frampton hired me a week ago. She thinks her husband's been cheating on her and she wants us to prove it. I've got all the background information in here, but what I want you to focus on is the photograph of her husband. You need to get to know that picture. In the dark it can be hard to make sure you've got the right man."

I studied the candid shot of a nice, ordinary-looking man in a suit. He was probably in his late thirties, clean-shaven, with brown hair.

"We're going to hang out at the home of his suspected girlfriend. If he shows up, we shoot some video. It's not complicated."

Was she kidding? I searched her expression for a hint of humor, but Erin really seemed to think this was all humdrum stuff.

Murphy arrived with the food. "Eat every bite," he admonished Erin, before leaving to serve another customer.

Here was advice that I agreed with. Erin was far too thin. Yet, she tucked into the sandwich with what seemed to be a healthy appetite.

I compared her plate to mine and too late I realized I'd made a mistake with the BLT. I'd never seen anything that looked as limp and greasy.

"So how do we do this?" I asked.

"Just pick it up and eat it. No fancy table manners required at Murphy's."

"No, I meant the stakeout. What do we do if a neighbor notices us hanging around?" They could call the police, and what would we do *then*?

"Neighbors are pretty clueless as a rule. But if they

do go so far as to phone in a complaint, I'll handle the cops, no problem." She cut into her sandwich then looked at me. "You aren't eating."

I nibbled at the tasteless white bread, fried with too much grease, not enough heat. Would it have killed the produce budget to add a thicker slice of tomato? I fought the urge to spit the food back onto the plate.

"Try some of this, honey." Erin pushed the ketchup bottle closer. "And next time you might want to order the steak sandwich."

"But I don't eat red meat."

Erin looked at me as if I was nuts. Then she snapped her fingers. "Ah. Because of Gary?"

"Well, actually…" I hated to admit it…. "Sort of." Eliminating red meat from the family's diet was the one concession I'd made when Gary had started demanding the family eat vegetarian.

Though I had to admit, the steak sandwich looked good. Or it would if I weren't so darn worried about my job.

"Are you sure I can do this, Erin?"

"You're talking about the job, right? Not the sandwich?"

"Right."

Erin put a hand on my arm. "You can do it. The hardest part is going for hours without peeing. You might want to consider bringing an empty plastic ice-cream container, just in case."

CHAPTER 3

Nine hours later, I met Erin back at Murphy's Grill. Shelley was spending the night at our place, with Devin and Jamie sharing babysitting responsibilities. Per Erin's instructions, I had brought a large insulated travel mug, but no ice-cream pail. I was hoping Erin had been joking about that. I placed my cup on the counter next to Erin's and watched as Murphy emptied the coffeepot into both of them.

Given the lack of washroom facilities, as previously outlined by Erin, I wasn't sure the super-sized coffees were such a great idea. But Erin seemed to think a person could never get enough of Murphy's coffee.

Even as I had that thought, Murphy's dark brown eyes settled on me. "Want room for cream?"

"Oh, yes. Lots of room, please."

Murphy paused, looked at me intently, then turned to Erin. "She has nice manners."

Erin seemed oddly proud. "Didn't I tell you?"

"What's going on with you two? Is it a crime to say *please* in this neighborhood?"

Erin ignored my question, just pushed the cream pitcher my way. "Okay, we're set. Let's make tracks."

Although it was dark outside, the temperature was still hot, the early August air oppressively muggy. I slipped into the passenger seat of Erin's Toyota and had no sooner inserted my mug into one of the cup holders than Erin handed me a package of batteries.

"Put those in the glove compartment, would you? Nothing worse than running out of batteries at just the wrong moment."

I unlatched the glove compartment. A flashlight rolled out to the floor. I groped in the dark, found it, then jammed everything back into place.

Erin already had the car in motion. She U-turned at the next intersection, now heading east on Dupont. The street was narrow with cars parked solidly on both sides—even at this time of night. I kept expecting us to clip off a few side mirrors, but Erin knew what she was doing.

"Okay, here's a little background," Erin said. "Our

client, Sherry, is a big-shot VP at one of the downtown banks and travels to New York a lot."

"She's there now?" I guessed.

"Yup. Left this morning. She's been worried for some time that her husband, Martin, has been sneaking around on her."

"Did she try asking him?"

Erin gave me a pitying look, as if she couldn't believe anyone could be so naive. "He denied it. Told Sherry he still loves her. But Sherry's pretty sure it's her six-figure income he's really crazy about."

Erin turned left on Spadina and as we passed Casa Loma, I peered out the window at the grand stone structure. "When the girls were little they used to love visiting this place."

"Yeah? I'll have to take Shelley sometime."

I was surprised Erin hadn't already done so, especially since the castle was close to where she lived. But then I thought about the admission rates, and the fact that Erin worked two jobs as well as looked after her daughter on her own.

We were now in the Forest Hill neighborhood, driving along winding roads bordered by majestic trees and gracious stone and brick mansions. Devin and Jamie's school was just up the way on Avenue Road, but Erin kept to the side streets. This was one of the few neighborhoods in Toronto that rivaled Rosedale, and I gazed out the window longingly.

"Nice, huh?" Erin said.

"Oh, yes." I wondered if Erin would be surprised to find out that until recently my girls and I had lived in a home just as splendid as these. We'd had so much, and now we had…

Enough. We had enough. I had to stop whining, even if it was just to myself.

"Where are we headed?" I checked out a street sign as we cruised slowly through the next intersection.

Erin recited the address.

"Martin's girlfriend must be well-off to live there."

"She should be. She's Sherry's boss."

"Her boss?"

Erin grinned, her crooked teeth gleaming in the light from the dash. "Kinky, isn't it?"

Now I really felt sorry for Sherry. Not only was her husband cheating on her, but so was her boss. Not that it was technically cheating in the boss's case, but it was certainly a betrayal.

Erin took her foot off the gas. "Here's the house."

It was a classic Tudor home, with lovely English-garden-styled landscaping.

"I scoped out the neighborhood earlier. We can park down the block. The people who live there have teens. Cars are always coming and going."

Erin pulled into a vacant space, opened her window a few inches, then motioned for me to do the same. "I know it's hot, but we can't run the air-conditioning. It'll look too suspicious."

"And two women sitting in a parked car won't?"

"You notice I picked a spot between streetlights. We're in the shadows here. Now, just recline your seat—" as she spoke, Erin demonstrated "—and no one will even see we're here."

There were all sorts of tricks to this game, I realized. "Are we sure Martin is going to show up tonight?"

"No."

That was disappointing. "What if he doesn't?"

"Then we come back tomorrow. Then the next night and the next."

"Sounds...boring."

Erin's grin flashed again. "Now you know why we needed the coffee. Without it, I'd fall asleep in the first hour."

"Good point."

"Can you pass me the camera? It's at your feet."

I found the vinyl bag and handed it over. "Is he

here?" A car had just driven by, but though it had seemed to slow a little, it hadn't stopped.

"Nah, I'm just getting prepared. Nothing bums me out more than waiting for hours, then missing the shot when something finally does happen."

I watched as Erin turned on the power, then inserted a fresh cassette into the machine. Funny how comfortable I felt, sitting in this car with a woman I'd known for only a week. Usually it took me a while to warm up to strangers. Yet, I'd confided the details of my marriage breakup to Erin within an hour of meeting her.

"You've heard my life story, but I know hardly anything about you. Have you lived in Toronto long?"

"All my life—just like you. Well, maybe not *just* like you. My mom had a house in the Beaches—that was before the yuppies declared the place trendy and drove up the real-estate prices."

"Must have been a fun place to be a kid." I had enjoyed taking the girls to the Beaches when they were little. We'd stroll along the boardwalk on the shore of Lake Ontario, then walk up to Queen Street for an ice-cream cone and a little window-shopping.

"It was fun, yeah, until my mother remarried."

I noted the injection of coolness into her tone. "You didn't like your stepfather?"

"You could say that. I beat it out of there as soon as I could land a job. After that, it was sort of my policy to make the stupidest choices I could possibly make."

All the while she'd been talking, Erin had been carefully scanning the road, passing cars and the occasional pedestrian. Now she let her gaze settle on mine for a second. "You name it, I've probably done it. The one good piece of luck I had is that I was never arrested. I wouldn't have been able to get my P.I. license if I had a record."

I wondered if I'd ever met anyone more unlike myself than Erin. You name it, I *hadn't* done it. I'd even refused to try marijuana when I was in college.

But then, so had Gary. We'd been such a straight couple. I'd thought that was one of the things that made us so perfect for each other. But perhaps our lack of adventurousness when we were younger was exactly why Gary was rebelling now.

Wait. I was thinking about Gary, and about our failed relationship again. I was supposed to stop doing that.

There was something else I wanted to ask Erin about. "How long have you known Murphy?"

"I met him the night I moved into the neighborhood, when Shelley was still a baby. After an exhausting day of moving I couldn't believe it when she wouldn't settle for the night. By midnight I was almost crazy. She just wouldn't stop crying."

"Colic?"

"Or something. Anyway, I was almost out of my mind and I decided, to hell with the breast-feeding rules, I needed coffee. I didn't have any in the house so I went to Murphy's. You have to understand that when I walked into that diner, the kid was yelling at the top of her lungs. I expected to be kicked out onto the street."

"But Murphy didn't kick you out."

"Nah. He poured me a cup of coffee, then came out from behind the counter and took Shelley into his arms. Damned if he didn't hold her right, too, supporting her head and all of that. The little monster had the nerve to shut right up. I kidded Murphy it was because she was scared, but she wasn't. She took to him on sight."

Erin shook her head, as if it defied belief, and I had to admit, Murphy did not seem like the nurturing sort. Still I wasn't surprised to find out that Murphy had a softer side. When he looked at Erin, it was clear that he cared about her.

"Are you and Murphy…?"

Erin's eyes widened. "No way. Not that I don't like the guy, you understand. It's just that by the time Shelley came into my life, I'd had enough of men. It's always been just the two of us, and that's how I want to keep things."

"But don't you ever—" I stopped talking as Erin lifted a finger to her lips.

"Shh." She turned the key to the auxiliary position, then lowered her window all the way down. As she did this, a dark sedan in front of us began to slow. The driver parked his car a discreet distance from Sherry's boss's place, then stepped out.

I scrunched as low in my seat as I could manage while still keeping an eye on the street. My heart was pounding so madly it was as if *I* was the one who was doing something wrong here, not Martin. I wondered if I would ever be able to do this job without feeling like a criminal.

The man we were pretty sure was Martin looked up and down the street. I was scared to death that he would spot us, but he seemed to find nothing amiss. He pocketed his keys then walked jauntily along the sidewalk headed for the Tudor house.

As he stepped under a street lamp, I got a clear view of his face. It was definitely Martin. Beside me, Erin switched on the camera and began training it on him.

Good thing Erin had remembered. I'd been so on edge, I hadn't even thought about the need to shoot video.

But, disappointingly, there wasn't much to capture on film. The front door opened and I caught only the briefest glimpse of a woman before Martin slipped inside and the door shut tightly again.

"Well, that was useless." So Martin had gone inside the house. We couldn't even prove he'd been met at the door by Sherry's boss. "Are you sure we shouldn't try and get some footage of the bedroom?"

Erin powered the camera off and returned it to the vinyl case. "Aside from the fact that the bedrooms are on the second story and I'm lousy at climbing trees, we probably won't need to. This camera prints the date and time of the footage. Let Martin try and explain why he was at this house so late on a Wednesday night."

"That is suspicious on its own right," I had to agree.

"Besides, we might get lucky when they're done. Usually cheaters are pretty cautious at the beginning of a date. But I've often caught a good hot kiss on the doorstep around midnight when they don't think anyone will be in sight."

"That makes sense." I hoped it would happen. I wanted Sherry to nail this jerk and teach him a lesson. Next time, Martin might think twice about cheating on a woman when he'd promised fidelity.

An hour went by. Then another. I had been so excited at the beginning of the evening, I hadn't been able to imagine feeling tired or, worse, nodding off. But after another hour passed, I started yawning. The coffee was gone, as was the bag of potato chips Erin had stashed in the back seat.

"Can we change the radio station?" Maybe a talk program would help me focus.

"Go ahead."

As I played with the controls, Erin grabbed the camera from the floor.

"What? Did I miss something?"

"No. I'm just guessing that they might be finishing soon. I think I'll get better pictures of the tender goodbye scene if I hide in that shrub over there." She pointed.

"The dogwood?"

"Whatever." Erin opened the car door, and after a brief hesitation, I followed her.

"You don't have to do this," Erin whispered. "Why don't you wait in the car and be comfortable?"

"No way." I was here to learn. Eventually I'd be doing this on my own and I wanted to do it right.

Erin hesitated, then passed me the camera. "You might as well do the shooting then." She paused by the shrub, then got down on her knees and crawled in among the branches.

I did the same, squirming around until I'd made myself reasonably comfortable. Once settled, I checked the controls of the camera, wanting to be familiar with how to operate it.

"See the door?" Erin said softly. "We have a better angle here. Even if they don't come out on the stoop, we should get some decent footage of the woman."

"Right." I was primed for action but, as minute followed minute, my adrenaline rush began to fade. I needed to talk or I was going to fall asleep.

"When did you get into the P.I. business, Erin?"

"About ten years ago I started working for this guy, Harvey Westman. He was quite a character, but he was mostly legit and he taught me the ropes. When he had a heart attack, I took over the business."

Something in Erin's voice suggested that this Harvey had been special to her. "Were you and Harvey friends?"

"Sure."

I hesitated. "More than friends?

"Harvey had twenty years on me."

Not a straight answer, which made me all the more curious. Could Harvey have been Shelley's father? I didn't quite dare to ask the question.

Erin's hand clamped on my arm a split second before I noticed the same thing she had. The front door to the Tudor home was opening. Martin stepped out to the landing and, as Erin had guessed, the woman gave him a goodbye kiss, right underneath the bright porch light.

I got it all on video, but couldn't manage to get a clear facial shot of either of them. Once the woman had gone back inside and Martin had driven off, I handed the camera back to Erin.

"I don't think that was very good."

"We tried. It just goes that way sometimes." She scrambled out of the bush and started pulling twigs from her hair.

As we walked back to her car, I asked what had happened to Harvey after his heart attack.

"He died," she said matter-of-factly. "He had no family and we were close, so he named me as his beneficiary—there was a will and everything. That's how I got the business…and enough money for a down payment on my house."

"Sounds like a good guy."

"Better than most."

Pretty cynical, I thought. Then again, my opinion of men wasn't much better these days. Maybe Erin and I had something in common after all.

CHAPTER 4

Though I didn't get home until after one, the next morning I forced myself out of bed in time to make the girls' lunches. Last night Erin had carried a sleeping Shelley home to her own bed, so it was just the three of us, as usual.

Devin was already at the table, eating her bowl of cereal. Five minutes later, when it was time to leave for the bus, Jamie rushed into the room.

"Do we have any muffins? My alarm clock didn't work. Mom, can you get me a new one?"

So easy to say, I reflected. And only a year ago, I would have added the item to my shopping list and picked one up at the Bay without a further thought.

"I'll take a look at it later. And yes, we have muffins." I passed her a bran one. "And here's your lunch."

Devin stuffed her sandwich, fruit and cookies into her knapsack without comment. Jamie stared at hers in disgust.

"I hate bringing a lunch to work. All the other swim instructors buy theirs."

I refused to feel guilty. "If a cafeteria lunch is that important to you, then buy it with your own money."

"Mom's lunches are better." Devin gave me a kiss, then headed for the door.

Jamie stared after her, lips curled dismissively. "She is such a suck."

My first instinct was to defend Devin. But I knew that would only escalate the sibling rivalry. So, I aimed for a lighter tone. "Come on, Jamie, admit it. You love Mommy's lunches, too."

Though Jamie shook her head and rolled her eyes, I saw a hint of a smile.

"Have a nice day, Mom. I'm out of here."

A few seconds later, the front door slammed, and I was alone in the house. I hesitated a moment, wondering if I should just crawl back into bed. I had the morning free since I wasn't meeting Erin to discuss our next case until one o'clock.

In the months after Gary left, I'd spent many mornings that way, tucked under the covers, trying not to think about how I was going to fill the hours until the girls came home from school. I didn't want to fall back into that pattern.

What I needed was coffee. I went to the cupboard and pulled out the tin of economy blend that I'd compromised on in an effort to keep the grocery bill under control.

I started to measure out the right number of scoops, but after the first one I stopped. The idea of sitting in this run-down kitchen by myself and gulping down a pot of cheap coffee was so unappealing.

A moment later I made my decision. Since the divorce, I'd given up Belgian chocolate, fashion magazines and organic produce. I was not going to give up my coffee, as well.

I'd had my heart set on something that combined coffee, chocolate, caramel sauce and whipped cream. Unfortunately, I could not find a café that sold specialty coffees anywhere in my new neighborhood. I still didn't want to go back to my lonely house, though. In resignation I found myself returning to Murphy's Grill.

At least I would fit in with the crowd better today, with my jeans and casual, though admittedly silk, T-shirt. When I'd been putting on my earrings, I'd thought about taking off my necklace, but pearls were supposed to go with anything so I'd left them on.

As I entered the small establishment I wasn't too surprised to find Erin seated at the counter facing the kitchen.

She twisted in her seat and gave a weary wave. "Why do kids have to wake up so bloody early?" She took a long swallow of her coffee.

I perched on the stool next to her, setting the alarm clock I'd brought with me on the counter. "I used to consider myself a morning person. Now, I'm not so sure. So where is Shelley?"

"Day camp at the community center."

Murphy emerged from the kitchen with two plates loaded with eggs, toast, bacon and hash browns. He hesitated for a second when he spotted me.

He'd shaved. And he looked good. Nice jaw, strong cheekbones. He was wearing a plaid shirt again, but a different one.

I wondered why I found him so attractive when he was completely different from any man I'd ever dated. Not that there'd been that many.

Maybe he got to me for the oldest reason in the book. Because I clearly didn't get to him. His indifference bugged me.

"Addicted already?" he said as he passed by on his way to his waiting customers.

I noticed they tucked into their breakfasts as if they hadn't seen food in a week.

"The breakfast special is the only other edible thing on the menu," Erin said, not seeming to care that she was speaking loudly enough for others—including Murphy—to hear.

Remembering my greasy BLT from yesterday, I asked, "The other being the steak sandwich? You could have warned me."

"Some lessons are better learned through experience," Erin replied.

Murphy was back behind the counter now. Leaving room for cream, he filled a mug with coffee, then slid it along the counter toward me before slipping back to the kitchen.

Erin pushed the cream pitcher closer and I did the necessary mixing, then took my first sip. Suddenly the crazy world seemed to come into focus. "I think coffee does for me what yoga does for Gary."

Beside me, Erin had both hands around her mug, holding it close as if she was afraid someone was going to try and grab it away. "You mean it takes you to another level of consciousness?"

"Yes. From asleep to awake."

Erin laughed. "You'll get used to the late nights."

"Will I?"

"Actually, no. Not as long as you've got kids at home."

"Only three more years for me," I said, not feeling as happy about that fact as I sounded. Sleeping in seemed like a small benefit when I thought about the prospect of living alone after all these years of raising a family.

Murphy passed by with two more plates of hot food. I glanced over at Erin. "Want to split a breakfast special?"

For the first time that morning, Erin opened her eyes all the way. "Are you crazy? Murphy *hates it* when people order things to share. Besides, I don't eat breakfast." She held out her empty mug as Murphy walked by with the pot in his hand. He refilled her coffee practically without breaking stride.

"You?" he asked me.

I shook my head. "I'm good."

Erin downed about half the coffee in her cup. "This is actually handy that we ran into each other. I have an appointment later this morning, so I can give you the keys for Adam's condo now."

She pulled them from her bag, along with a sheet of paper with an address.

I took both items and stowed them in my purse. "Um… What do I do with these?"

"Remember how I said that the company was called *Creative* Investigations?"

I so did not like that question. "Yes?"

"Well, I was talking to this woman the other week. Shelley was getting her teeth cleaned. This woman was the hygienist. Her name is Ava."

So far, so good. I nodded for her to go on.

"Turns out Ava has a big crush on the dentist in her office. She's been working there for a few months but he hasn't shown any interest, yet."

"Maybe he doesn't date his employees." Which seemed like a smart policy to me.

"Ava doesn't want him to date her. She wants him to marry her."

"But— She's only known him a few months. How can she be so sure?"

"She just is. Anyway, we were talking, and she told me that he'd recently lost his cleaning lady. He was asking the staff for recommendations."

None of this was computing so far. "I did have a

cleaning lady, but she's very in demand. I'm sure she's filled my slot by—"

"That's not it, Lauren. We aren't *looking* for a cleaning service. We *are* the cleaning service."

I *still* didn't get it.

"Here's the plan. We go into Adam's condo every two weeks. We find out what he's reading, what movies he's rented, his favorite flavor of ice cream. Then Ava uses this information to convince him that they're perfect soul mates."

Erin leaned back on her stool and gave a satisfied smile.

"That's a perfect plan?"

"What don't you like about it?"

"Well, first off…who cleans Adam's condo?"

"We do."

"You mean, *I* do."

"Well, yeah, but you get to keep the extra hundred bucks. See, that's the beauty of this arrangement. Ava pays us to get the goods on Adam. And Adam pays us to clean."

So I wasn't really a private investigator. I was a glorified maid. On the positive side, at least I knew how to vacuum and clean toilets.

"But it all seems so…"

"Creative?"

"I was thinking illegal, actually."

"You worry too much, Lauren. This is the perfect gig. And it's all yours. Adam wants his place cleaned on Tuesday afternoon and I've already got a regular job scheduled for that time."

Oh, lucky me.

"Keep on the lookout for signs of a regular girl-friend. According to Ava, he's never mentioned one at the office, but you never know."

"By signs you mean women's clothing, that sort of thing?"

"Yeah. Check for an extra toothbrush, women's toi-letries, the regular girlie stuff."

"And when I'm done?"

"Write up a report. Ava will want to pick it up in person. She has roommates and we obviously can't send it to the office. Wouldn't want this stuff in the wrong hands."

Definitely not. Wouldn't want the wrong girl becoming the dentist's soul mate.

"Okay, you're set." Erin tossed a toonie on the counter for her coffee. Halfway to the door, she stopped and looked back at me. "You don't have to do this. I could tell Ava I couldn't fit her in."

I was tempted to tell her to do just that. Then my eyes fell on the broken alarm clock on the counter. I thought about the gap in my budget between expenditures and income. "I'm okay with it."

"Good. You'll do fine." Erin grinned. "Though I've got to admit I'm having a hard time picturing you cleaning someone else's toilet."

I grimaced while she laughed at me. That was actually the only part of the job I didn't object to. I wondered how Ava was going to feel ten years from now when she was married to a man she had nothing in common with.

Once Erin had left, I dug out the change to cover my own cup of coffee. As I dumped it on the counter, Murphy walked up from behind me.

"Is it broken?" He picked the alarm clock off the counter and looked it over.

"My daughter says it is. I thought maybe at the hardware store Denny could give me the name of someone—"

"You'll end up getting charged enough money to buy a new one."

Yes. He was probably right. I'd have to use part of the extra hundred dollars I was going to earn this afternoon to buy a replacement. I held out my hand to take it back, but Murphy ignored me.

"Our garbage dumps are full enough. Leave this with me and I'll take a look at it. It's probably something simple."

"But—" Why would he offer to do something like this? I really hadn't thought he liked me at all. Was it possible he truly was offering out of concern for the environment? "Thank you. I'll pay you for your time."

"Yeah? I wouldn't make that offer if I was you." He waved a hand at me. "Now get out of here. I've got customers waiting for that stool."

He didn't, the place was half-empty, but I left as requested.

At twelve-thirty, I took the bus to the subway and rode to the St. George stop. When we'd first moved to Dovercourt Village, I hadn't taken the subway in years and had forgotten that the concept of personal space was meaningless on public transport. Now I was becoming accustomed to the smell of strangers again, and the distinction between the sway of the bus versus the rocking motion of the subway.

The truly great thing about transit, however, was never needing to worry about finding a parking space or encountering a snarl in traffic. When I emerged from the subway station, cars were at a standstill or both sides of the street. I blithely walked past the jam and headed north to the dentist's condo.

With Erin's piece of paper in hand, I stopped in front of an elegant stucco building and consulted the address again.

Yes, this was the right place.

I followed the brick path to the front security door. A well-dressed woman exiting the complex gave me a frown, then paused to make sure the door had closed completely before leaving me on the stoop.

I made a show of pulling out my keys. She glared.

"I'm the new cleaning lady for unit two."

Clearly she didn't believe me. I tucked my pearls back under the cotton T-shirt I'd worn for the gig, then slipped my key into the lock, praying it would work.

It did.

Ironically, just as I'd proven I had a legitimate reason to be here, I felt like the criminal that woman had obviously thought I might be.

This was so crazy. I was about to enter the house of a perfect stranger.

Cleaning ladies do it all the time.

Yes, but cleaning ladies don't check for extra toothbrushes. They don't make lists of their client's reading materials and examine the contents of their kitchen cupboards. At least, they aren't supposed to.

So you're a snoopy cleaning lady. There's no law against snooping.

Okay, technically I wasn't breaking the law. But ethically speaking, I was still about to do something wrong.

If you're going to be a wuss about this, maybe you should look for a different job.

I let the door close behind me. I was inside.

The building's foyer was spotless and fortunately deserted. I followed the hallway to the left. Adam's unit was the second one. As I let myself in, I heard a door farther down the hall open, then shut again.

A nosy neighbor? I closed Adam's door behind me with relief.

The hardest part was over. At least I didn't have to worry that anyone was watching me in here.

I surveyed the foyer, which was surprisingly tidy for a single man living on his own. All the coats were hung in the closet. A gym bag sat on a footstool next to an umbrella rack. Shoes were organized in a neat line on the floor under the jackets.

At least he was neat. But then, he was a dentist— what did I expect?

The rest of the condo was also neat, but not particularly clean. The blinds were coated with dust and the grout in the shower was suspiciously black.

I wondered how long it had been since Adam's previous cleaning lady had quit. But that was at least a year's worth of dust on the blinds. Which meant Adam didn't keep very close tabs on his cleaning lady.

That should have been good news. It meant that I didn't need to worry about doing a top-notch job.

Unfortunately, I didn't think I could live with myself if I snooped *and* shirked my cleaning duties. Which meant I was going to be working very hard for my hundred dollars today.

CHAPTER 5

By the time I made it home after cleaning Adam's condo, it was already five o'clock. Jamie was prowling the kitchen on the search for something to make for dinner. A new postcard from her father had been tossed on the kitchen table.

Casually, I picked it up. Unsurprisingly, the photograph was of a temple. Since his arrival in India, Gary's postcards had been either street scenes showing improbable combinations of cars, elephants, cows, motorcycles and stray dogs—or religious monuments.

I flipped the card over. Gary's tiny, cramped writing covered every available blank space.

Well, I'm finally in Chennai.

I'm. He never referred to the woman he was traveling with in his correspondence with the girls. I could only assume that they were still together.

Yesterday was my first visit to the Krishnam-acharya Yoga Mandiram (KYM). Very impress-ive and not at all like the yoga studios at home. Remember how you complained when I took you to try a class once, Devin? Here they teach that yoga is adapted to the person, not the per-son to yoga. I thought that might encourage you to give it another shot.

Jamie, I wish you could try all the wonderful food they have here. My current favorite is a doughnut called *vada*. It's made from mashed lentils and is delicious with a hot cup of chai.

One day, girls, I'll bring you here so you can experience all this yourself.

He signed off the way he always did: *Love to you and your mother, Dad.*

I dropped the postcard back on the table. I was well aware that while Jamie appeared to be fascinated by the contents of the fridge, she was watching me closely for my reaction.

"Those *vadas* sound good," I said, hoping I had

achieved the right note of casual interest in my voice. "I wonder if we can get them here."

"Mashed lentils? Yuck. No thanks." She slammed the fridge closed. "Can we have waffles and creamed eggs for dinner?"

"Maybe." I sighed. I knew the girls were angry at their father. I couldn't really blame them. Gary claimed to love them. But to a couple of fifteen-year-olds, the words sounded a little hollow coming from the other side of the globe.

"When will dinner be ready?"

In my mind I calculated the time to boil eggs, mix waffle batter and make a white sauce. "In about thirty minutes."

Jamie said nothing to that, just disappeared to her room. I wished I could do the same. All day long my cozy bed had been calling to me, but never more than right now. Despite having worked at a crazy pace for almost three hours, I hadn't been able to do more than regular cleaning at Adam's, plus the refrigerator. At this rate, it was going to take me months to get the place into proper shape.

I put a pot of water on the stove, then went to the fridge for eggs. Footsteps thundered down the stairs and Jamie rushed back into the kitchen.

"Hey, Mom. I forgot to tell you. Erin phoned a while ago and invited us for dinner. Do we have to go?"

"She invited us for dinner…tonight?"

"Yeah. But I'd rather stay here."

I didn't exactly feel like going out either. On the other hand, I wouldn't have to cook… "Did she say what time?"

"She said whenever."

I had never experienced such a casual attitude to a dinner invitation. But tonight it might be my salvation.

"I have lessons to prepare," Jamie added. But I wasn't fooled. For Jamie, preparing lessons, like homework, equaled eighty-percent time spent on the phone and MSN with friends, twenty-percent actual reading and writing time.

"If you want dinner, then yes, you have to come to Erin's. You can excuse yourself early to do your lesson planning if you like. Where's your sister?"

"In her room."

"Go get her please. I'll grab a bottle of wine." Since Gary hadn't been able to take it with him to India, I had ended up with the contents of our wine cellar in the downstairs storage room. I might not be able to afford to feed our children, but we would always have wine for the table.

As soon as the twins were ready, we headed next door. We were greeted with the rich aroma of curry and very loud music.

"God, it smells good in here," Jamie said.

Devin looked impressed, too. "Black Eyed Peas. Cool."

"Is that what's cooking?" I went to the stove where Erin was stirring the contents of a large pot.

"God, Mom." Devin sounded mortified.

"She was talking about the music," Erin explained, looking mildly amused. "This is lentil stew."

"It smells great. Thanks so much for the invite. The last thing I felt like doing tonight was cook."

"I figured as much. I'm always exhausted when I finish cleaning my place." Erin glanced at the girls, hovering near the doorway. "Get in here and help yourself to something to drink. I've got coolers in the fridge."

Coolers? Alcoholic coolers?

Jamie went to the fridge and pulled out two bottles, one peach flavored, one strawberry. She opened them both, then offered her sister a choice. Devin glanced at me for approval before she took it.

I hesitated, then nodded. The girls were four years from the legal drinking limit, but with all the madness of our lives lately, I figured an alcoholic drink at home, with their mother in the house, wasn't such a big deal.

"You brought wine? Great. The corkscrew is in that drawer." Erin pointed with the wooden spoon. Then she turned to the girls. "If you want to pick out something to listen to next, my CDs are in the living room."

"Sweet."

The girls left and I took a closer look at the stew. Simmering in a savory sauce were lentils, chickpeas, cauliflower, carrots and onions. Remembering Jamie's earlier comment about mashed lentils, I hoped the girls would eat a little, and be polite about it.

The doorbell rang.

"Lauren, would you get that? It's probably Lacey. I told her to come over when she finished with bingo."

"Sure." I passed through the hall to the front of the house. I could smell the cigarette smoke as soon as I opened the door.

Lacey didn't seem surprised to see me. She pushed her glasses up on her nose, then sniffed. "Lentil stew?"

"Yes."

"Good. It's my favorite."

To my surprise, all of us enjoyed Erin's meal, even Devin and Jamie. They had two servings each of the curry and devoured the side salad of spinach, orange and mixed nuts.

I had always considered my girls picky eaters. Had they changed without my noticing?

Or maybe it was the party atmosphere in Erin's house that made the difference. The coolers and the loud music. The conversations that wound through several topics, going nowhere yet everywhere at the same time. Lacey drank three coolers, while Erin and I polished off the bottle of wine.

Later, when the dishes had been cleared and the girls were debating which movie to watch—lesson plans long forgotten—I excused myself to use the washroom.

Just as at my place, Erin only had one, at the top of the stairs. She'd painted the exterior of her claw-foot tub a paprika color and she'd covered the old plumbing under the sink with a skirt of the same color. As I washed my hands, I noticed that Erin had a much bigger medicine cabinet than we did.

The pine-and-glass fixture obviously wasn't original to the house. I guessed it might have come from a place like IKEA. I wondered if Erin had installed it herself, and whether I would be able to handle a similar project. The girls and I could sure use the extra storage space.

Curious to have a look at the interior, I pulled at

the door. It wouldn't budge. Was it stuck on something?

A closer look revealed a tiny hook and latch, with a small lock holding the two together. So much for snooping inside Erin's medicine cabinet. With a little child in the house, she was probably wise to keep it locked, anyway.

The next day I worked all morning to prepare the report for Ava. The plan was to meet at noon at Murphy's and though I set out ten minutes early, when I arrived, Murphy's eyes were right on me as if I was late. He nodded his head toward a woman in the far corner, a petite redhead in her light blue hygienist's uniform.

"Ava?" I asked him.

He nodded again. "Want coffee?"

"Please." I headed for my client, drawing in a deep breath as I advanced. This was it. My first professional consultation. I was terrified that Ava would see right through me. *You're not a private investigator, you're just a mother and a housekeeper.*

I could feel my throat drying up, my palms getting damp. *Fake it, Lauren.* I held out my right hand. "Ava? Hi, I'm Lauren Holloway, Erin Karmeli's new partner."

To my amazement, Ava didn't challenge me. She shook my hand and thanked me for meeting her.

I sat next to her, placing my briefcase on the counter between us. Ava stared at it, fascinated, then lifted her eyes to mine. "Did everything go okay yesterday?"

"Smooth as silk," I assured her.

"Coffee," Murphy said from behind me.

I shifted to one side to make room for him to set the mug on the counter. "Thanks." He passed me the pitcher of cream and a spoon, then disappeared.

I pulled the report out of my briefcase, then doctored my coffee as Ava read it. I'd listed the current books on Adam's night table and the titles of movies he'd ordered that month from his cable bill.

I'd also accessed the laptop computer in his office. It had been surprisingly easy. Adam listed all his passwords in an address book he kept on the desk beside his laptop.

In the electronic in-box, I'd found a confirmed order for more books, movies and CDs from Amazon. I'd also seen a file labeled Fun. I'd opened it, then closed it quickly when I realized it contained porn.

I'd decided there was no need to include that information in Ava's report.

But I had included details about Adam's taste in

wine, cheese and take-out food. This was all I'd found in his refrigerator. He did have good quality pots and pans, knives and kitchen utensils, though, so I assumed he did cook on occasion.

"Did you see any sign of a woman in his life?" Ava asked.

"Not at all." There'd been only one toothbrush in the glass in his bathroom and absolutely no feminine beauty or grooming products.

Ava gave a small, satisfied smile. "Good."

I sipped my coffee and wondered what made this woman tick. Ava was pretty, young and in good shape. She shouldn't have any trouble getting dates. Why go to all this effort for this particular man?

"Adam must be a pretty special guy."

"He definitely is." Ava folded my report and tucked it into her snappy green handbag. "And soon he's going to be *my* guy. I'm going straight to the bookstore after I leave here to get that book he just ordered."

Guns, Germs, and Steel didn't sound too interesting to me. I was glad I wasn't after the dentist.

I finished my coffee and set the empty mug on the counter. "Well, I guess we're finished here."

"That was great, Lauren. Just what I needed." Ava handed me an envelope.

Though Erin had told me that Ava would be settling her account in cash, I stared at the envelope for a moment before I realized this was my payment. I felt strange accepting it, a little bit guilty as if I'd just concluded an illegal drug deal.

Ava stood, smoothed her slacks over her hips. "I'm on lunch break so I should be going. I guess I'll see you in two weeks. Unless I'm dating Adam by then." She winked, then put enough money on the counter to cover both coffees and then some.

"Thanks again, Lauren. These days a girl can use every advantage she can get."

Ava left. I stayed for a refill. My guilt was subsiding, being replaced by something I hadn't expected, something that felt suspiciously like elation.

I'd done it. Concluded my first solo investigative assignment. Maybe to others it wouldn't seem like such a big deal, but for the first time since Gary had left me, I finally felt as if I could handle life on my own.

Gary? Who needed him?

I, Lauren Anderson Holloway, P.I., was just fine on my own, thank you.

Passing by to clear up after a departing customer, Murphy gave me a cursory glance. "You look pleased with yourself."

"The meeting went well."

"Really?"

"You don't have to sound so surprised."

He shrugged. "Maybe Erin was right to hire you after all."

After all? "Did she talk to you about it?"

"We talk about a lot of things."

I felt an ugly twist of emotion and realized it was jealousy. For some reason I envied the relationship between Erin and Murphy, even though I didn't understand it. All I knew was that they were close…and that bugged me.

But why? It wasn't as if I wanted to be friends with Murphy. We had nothing in common. And though he was sexy, in that bad-boy way of his, he wasn't at all my type.

"You warned her not to hire me," I guessed. Right from the beginning I'd sensed, not so much that he didn't like me, but that he didn't approve of me.

And why did I care, when I'd already established that this man meant nothing to me?

"Hey, it's a lot of work to train a new employee. I just didn't want her to waste her time if you weren't going to stick."

"Why did you think I wouldn't stick?"

He looked me up and down dismissively. "I know you. I know your type. You're not going to last one year in this neighborhood."

I had to laugh. He was unbelievable. "If only that were true."

"Wait and see."

"You're crazy." I shook my head. "That's what I get for asking a stupid question."

I was about to leave, when he called me back.

"Hang on. I have something of yours." He reached under the counter and pulled out Jamie's alarm clock. "It was the ribbon connector on the display board. No big deal to fix."

I stared at him, totally confused. Talk about blowing hot and cold. "But—"

He turned on his heel and disappeared into the kitchen before I could even thank him.

CHAPTER 6

"How did things go with Ava?" Erin pushed a chair on wheels over the polished wood floor toward me.

It was later that night, Shelley was asleep and the twins had gone home to work on their end of session report cards. Erin and I were in the office of Creative Investigations, otherwise known as the third bedroom of Erin's home. She had a computer in here and all the usual accoutrements, like a fax machine, a printer and, of course, a shredder.

I steadied the chair, then sat down. "Fine." I dug in my briefcase for the envelope Ava had given me. "Here's the payment."

"Awesome." Erin removed a ring of keys from a drawer, then unlocked the filing cabinet and popped the envelope into a folder. "You look happy."

"I know it's silly, but it just feels so *good*. I thought I was going to have to get a job in retail. Or maybe work as a receptionist. I never imagined myself as a private investigator. And getting paid today...well that just made it seem so real."

"It is real. But maybe not so exciting as you think."

"Compared to my previous life, this has been pretty cutting-edge."

"That's because I lured you in with the dramatic stuff up front. Now I'm going to show you how we pay the bills." She lifted a file folder off her desk and passed it to me.

"Huh?"

"Background checks."

"For who?" In order to volunteer at the girls' school, every two years I had to sign a consent form to have one of these performed on me. It had never occurred to me that one day I might be the one doing the checking.

"Prospective employees of the Toronto College of Business Administration Studies. We have other clients, too, but they're our biggest."

"Wow. That sounds impressive. How did you land that account?"

"Sometimes my shady past pays off," Erin said mysteriously. "Let's just say, I know a lot of people."

I knew a lot of people, too. But I had a feeling none of them were going to be much use in this new life of mine.

On the other hand…adultery, fraud and deceit were pretty universal. Maybe I should print up some business cards and pass them around the old country club.

"I usually spend one or two days a week on background checks," Erin said. "By and large the work is routine. I have a checklist. Follow that and you can't go wrong."

I opened the folder and saw a typewritten sheet titled Procedures for Conducting Background Checks. It was eight pages long. "Looks like a very thorough check."

"Before the college makes a job offer, we make sure that the applicant has been honest about their employment history, education and other accreditations. Once the conditional offer of employment is accepted, we go on to check for any criminal history or a listing on the sexual and violent offender registry."

"I assume the prospective employees sign a consent form?"

"Absolutely. You want to make sure you have a copy of the Background Check Consent Statement in the file before you do anything."

Erin picked up a business card from her desk. "Here's the name of our contact in the HR department in case you need to talk to him about anything."

I accepted the card, then looked at the name. *Graham Irving.* I wondered if this guy meant anything to Erin. Could *he* be Shelley's father?

Erin continued to talk business, not giving me any opening to probe her personal life.

"As I said," she continued, "this is fairly routine stuff. Most people are exactly who they say they are. But every now and then you run across a screwball who just had to add an extra degree to their list of qualifications."

"What about criminals? Have you ever come across any of those?"

"It's rare, but it happens. A record for drug possession doesn't raise too many eyebrows. But if there's a sex crime in your past, well, different story."

"I can imagine." I rifled through the pile of papers apprehensively. Would I find a criminal in this batch?

"The good thing about this work is that we can do it from home. All you need is a phone and high-speed Internet."

I was set then. "There's a lot more to this P.I. business than I would have guessed."

"We're just scratching the surface," Erin assured me. "Once you've mastered the fine skill of background checks, I'm going to start taking you around the city to meet all my contacts. One thing you'll learn pretty quickly...an investigator is only as good as the people she knows."

"It's overwhelming."

"Yeah, I know. My first few months with Harvey, I felt like I was on crack or something. My head was always buzzing."

I wondered if Erin knew what crack was like based on personal experience. Probably. Did she still use illegal drugs? I was afraid to ask. But that might explain her pasty coloring and excessive thinness.

And it also might explain why the medicine cabinet in her bathroom was locked....

Don't be ridiculous, Lauren. The real explanation was certainly the most obvious, banal one. Erin was thin thanks to a fast metabolism rate and she kept the medicine cabinet locked because she was a cautious mother.

This P.I. business was going to my head.

It became routine for me to meet Erin for a morning coffee at Murphy's after I'd seen the girls off for the day. I wasn't sure why this happened. I still didn't like Murphy's coffee. And Murphy still didn't seem to like me.

But the house was so empty when the girls were gone. And it gave Erin and me a chance to discuss our work schedules for the day.

On the last Monday of August my morning was especially chaotic. Jamie had a lifeguarding shift to cover but she'd neglected to empty her gym bag from last week and all her bathing suits were damp. I had to negotiate an agreement between the twins whereby Jamie could borrow one of Devin's suits for the day, if Jamie would chip in half the cost for a new CD Devin wanted.

When I finally arrived at Murphy's, I was about fifteen minutes later than usual. Erin was at the counter talking quietly, yet intently, to Murphy. They were so close their heads seemed to be touching.

The moment Murphy spotted me, though, he pulled back. He said something to Erin and she turned around in her seat to wave me over.

I *knew* they had been talking about me. Was Murphy still trying to convince Erin she'd made a mistake hiring me? I couldn't understand why he cared. He claimed to be worried that I wouldn't stay in the neighborhood, but even if I won the lottery and was able to afford someplace better, would it really be such a big deal?

Surely Erin could find someone else to do the job. It wasn't like I had any special qualifications in the first place.

"What's up?" I asked as I joined them.

"Not much," Erin said.

There was a deliberate blankness in her eyes that confirmed my suspicions. Darn it, they *had* been talking about me.

I knew she and Murphy were good friends, but still I didn't like it. After all, Erin and I worked together now. We'd had dinner at each other's houses, knew each other's kids, had watched a few movies in the evenings and drunk more than a few bottles of wine together.

We were friends, too, weren't we?

Murphy slid me a cup, filled it with coffee.

I remembered something that had been slipping my mind every morning lately. "Thanks for fixing the alarm clock. Jamie's actually waking up on time now."

"No problem."

He met my gaze briefly, and I felt a lingering resentment. There was something about this man that grated...but also intrigued. He didn't look me in the eyes very often, but when he did, I felt as if I was staring into the soul of the big, bad wolf...and liking it.

That was what was so annoying. Despite Murphy making no secret of the fact that I was far from his favorite person, something about the man kept drawing me.

I eyed a breakfast special as the cook set it on the ledge separating the kitchen from the serving area. I hadn't had time to eat this morning and experience had taught me that it wasn't wise to drink Murphy's coffee on an empty stomach.

"I think I'll have the breakfast this morning. It doesn't come in half orders, does it?"

Murphy folded his arms over his chest. "No."

"Well, I won't be able to eat all that food. What if I pay the same price, but you just cut back—"

"No."

I rolled my eyes. Why was he being so obstinate about this? "Fine. Waste food then. It doesn't matter to me."

I sipped at my coffee as Murphy placed my order with the kitchen.

"How are those background checks going?" Erin asked.

"No problems so far." In fact, I was a little disappointed that I hadn't turned up anything exciting. The routine desk work hadn't dimmed my enthusiasm about the new job though.

Becoming a private investigator was probably the last job I would have picked for myself and that was exactly why I loved it. Now that I was out of my Rosedale house, no longer linked to the community where I had thrived for so long, I realized I needed to embrace new directions.

Like romance? My gaze fell on Murphy as he used his shoulders to open the swinging door to the kitchen. *Nice shoulders.*

I glanced discreetly over at Erin, to see if she'd noticed, too. Erin wasn't paying any attention to Murphy, though. Not at the moment. She was stirring her coffee, looking thoughtful.

"I didn't interrupt something earlier, did I?"

"What?" Erin sounded confused by the question.

"When I came into the diner just now, you and Murphy seemed to be in your own little world. I wondered if maybe—you know—*maybe?*"

Amusement added a spark of life to Erin's eyes. "I've

already told you, there's nothing hot and heavy between Murph and me. We're just friends."

"On a good day," Murphy added from behind her.

Erin started, almost lost her balance. "Why do you always do that? Sneak up out of nowhere?"

"You want to talk about me, don't do it in my diner." He whisked by us, taking a stack of dirty dishes to the kitchen. A minute later he returned with my breakfast.

Despite my claim that I couldn't eat all that food, I made a pretty good job of it. I tried to share with Erin, but all I could talk her into accepting was half a slice of toast.

Erin only ate a few bites, though, before setting it down. The other night, at dinner, she hadn't eaten much, either. The possibility had occurred to me before and now I entertained it again…could Erin be anorexic?

I took a bite of sausage and tried to steer my thoughts in a different direction. As my daughters would say, *Chill, Mom.* Why did I persist in thinking there had to be some explanation for Erin's thinness? I should be so lucky as to have a problem like that.

Over coffee refills, Erin and I hashed out the jobs we needed to take care of that day. I waited until we were walking home to take another stab at finding out what she and Murphy had been talking about earlier.

"You and Murphy seemed to be having a pretty intense conversation this morning."

"He worries about me, not that there's anything to worry about."

"Maybe he cares about you more than you know."

Erin gave me a curious look. "You keep insinuating that there's something going on between us. I assure you, there isn't."

"He isn't your type?"

"I told you before…after Shelley, I swore off men."

"Yes, but you don't mean *permanently?*"

Erin shrugged. "I overdosed on men when I was younger. You're looking at my clothes. Wondering why I dress this way?"

"Well…yes, a little." Almost every time I saw her, Erin was in tight jeans or short skirts. If she really didn't want to attract men, why wear clothing that emphasized her sexuality?

"A girl can do a lot of manipulating if she shows a little boob and a lot of leg."

I stared at her, not sure how to respond.

"Sounds cynical, I know, but that's how it is. How

about you, Lauren? Are you anxious to get back into the dating scene?"

Though I'd just had a similar thought myself, my instinctive reaction was to recoil. "God, no." Dating? I couldn't imagine it.

"Don't sound so outraged. It'll happen soon, you know," Erin predicted. "Women like you are never single for long."

"Women like me?"

"You know what I mean."

But I didn't. I didn't have a clue. What kind of woman was I? What would the average man on the street think when he met me?

"Murphy's worried I'm going to run out on you."

"Yeah, I know. Ignore him. He's very protective of me and Shelley."

Again, I felt a sense of disconnect. It didn't make sense that Murphy would be this concerned about one of Erin's employees.

"I don't understand that guy," I said. "He acts like he couldn't care less, yet the other day he fixed Jamie's alarm clock for free. I didn't even ask."

"He's handy with electronic gadgets."

"Come on, Erin."

"Okay, he's a sucker for women raising kids on

their own. Can't resist helping one if he can. His older sister had kids when she was just nineteen. Maybe that's why."

Murphy had a sister. Why did that seem so incongruous? Everyone had family. Even misanthropic loners. "Where's his sister now?"

Erin looked like she didn't want to answer, but finally she did. "His sister is gone. So are the kids."

"Gone?"

"As in dead."

"What?" I couldn't breathe for a moment.

"It happened a long time ago. There was a house fire. All of them died, including Murphy's mother."

"No." I stopped in the middle of the street we'd been crossing. "That's too awful."

Erin took my arm and dragged me to the sidewalk. "It gets worse. The fire wasn't an accident. Murphy's father's been incarcerated for about ten years now, serving time for arson and murder."

CHAPTER 7

"How old was Murphy when that happened?" I asked.

"Seventeen."

Lord. Just two years older than my girls.

"He was six months from graduating high school. But he never did. After the cops arrested his father, he went to live with his grandfather on his mother's side."

"I can't imagine going on after something like that. Poor Murphy."

"Poor grandfather, if you ask me. If you think Murphy's cantankerous now, can you imagine what he must have been like then? Plus, I don't think he was too happy moving from a house to a small apartment over a diner."

"Diner? Are you talking about the same one?"

"Sure. It belonged to his grandfather. Murphy Senior."

"What happened to the grandfather?"

"He died about ten years ago."

"How did you find out all this? Did Murphy tell you?"

"Are you kidding? Murphy hates to talk about himself."

"From what I've seen, Murphy hates to talk, period."

"You've got a point. Anyway, there are regulars who've been going to Murphy's for decades. One of them is Stan Murdock. He's in his seventies, uses a cane and wears a black tweed cap...."

I immediately knew who she was talking about. Though we'd never exchanged names, I'd spoken to him briefly a few times. "He's at Murphy's a lot."

"He is. If you notice, he's one of the few customers Murphy doesn't try to hustle out the door."

Erin was another.

"Thanks for telling me all this. It explains a lot." We'd been standing in front of our homes for the last few minutes and now I turned my attention to our joined houses, trying to be objective. Even with the small homey touches we'd each made—Erin's wicker furniture and flowers, and my rattan rocking chair and ivy door wreath—the house looked shabby.

It needed new siding and double-paned windows. An inviting front door wouldn't have hurt.

I sighed. No way could I afford any of those. And I had a feeling my neighbor couldn't either.

It was so strange that I, who had always been so careful to do the "right" things in life, and Erin, who openly admitted to deliberately making the "wrong" choices, had ended up at this exact same point in our lives: low-income single mothers in cheap housing, struggling to raise our children as best as we could.

Was it just our circumstances that were drawing us together? Yet, I felt comfortable around Erin, as if I could say anything and not be censured for it. It was a very unfamiliar feeling.

"Erin?"

"Yeah?" She'd been just about to disappear inside.

"Would you and Shelley like to come for dinner tonight?"

"Are you kidding? Of course we would."

"Good. I'll make roast beef."

"Red meat?" Erin made a face of mock horror. "I thought you gave that up?"

"We were out shopping the other day and Devin ordered a burger. I think it's time I stopped letting Gary dictate the family menu."

Pretending to choke, Erin let herself into the house, leaving me laughing on the street.

In between making Internet queries and phone calls for my background checks that day, I went shopping, peeled potatoes and prepared a broccoli casserole to go with the roast. As the day progressed, I found my mood growing more and more cheerful. I didn't even know why until Devin came home.

"Yum. It finally smells like home in here."

I finished covering the roast with foil to keep it warm. I'd managed to cook it to a perfect medium rare. "You're right, Devin. It does."

We tended to eat a lot of stir-fries and pastas. I hadn't prepared a traditional meal like this since... well, since Gary had gone vegetarian.

Devin lifted a corner of the foil and tore off a snippet of meat. "I bet even Jamie won't be able to resist this."

Shortly after Gary had moved out, Jamie had announced that she was turning vegetarian, too. I hadn't been sure how to take her decision. It had felt like a defection, but maybe I'd been too sensitive.

Jamie came in then and dumped her backpack on the floor. "Why does it stink in here?"

Or maybe not.

The back door hadn't fully closed, when it started to open again. Erin stuck her head inside. "We hopped the back fence—which is falling down, by the way—then followed our noses. Have I died and gone to heaven or is that a prime rib roast I smell?"

"Come on in," I said. "Shelley, would you like a taste?"

Shelley was no longer shy around me or my girls. She accepted the small slice of meat I offered, then ran over to Jamie.

"I like your fingernails."

Jamie had painted them with tiny yellow flowers.

"Would you like me to paint your nails, too?"

"I'll do your hair," Devin added. "It'll be like a spa day."

Had my girls offered Shelley a trip to Disneyland, she couldn't have looked happier.

"Yes, please!"

"Okay, then." Jamie bent down so Shelley could climb up on her back.

"Mom, can I take some sodas upstairs?" Devin asked before grabbing three cans from the fridge.

Watching them exit en masse, I smiled. "Isn't it nice that—" I caught a glimpse of Erin's face before she turned her back to me. She'd looked like she'd been about to cry. "What's wrong?"

"Nothing." Erin smiled, with obvious effort. "I just feel badly sometimes that Shelley is an only kid."

She was such a softy, Erin, for all her hip, tough attitude.

"I was an only child," I said. "I turned out okay."

"Yeah, you're okay, all right." Erin scanned the kitchen counter, making a quick recovery from her little meltdown. "Now what can I do to help? Just don't ask me to carve, make gravy or mash potatoes. I suck at all of those things."

"In that case, why don't you grab the bottle of red on the table and open it?"

"My specialty." She went to the table. "Say, guess what I discovered in one of my background checks today?"

We chatted business while I put the final touches on the meal. When it was ready, I called the girls down. Shelley marched into the dining room like a queen, holding out her hands, fingers splayed.

"Look, Mom! Aren't I pretty?"

"The prettiest." Erin bent to give the little girl a hug, being careful not to muss the braids or the polish.

Everyone ate with gusto, and I was amused to see that Devin had been right. After the first helpings had been taken, Jamie slipped a slice of roast beef to her plate. She also added a dollop of gravy to her potatoes when she thought no one was paying attention.

I looked around the table with satisfaction. One of the hardest things to adjust to after the divorce had been that empty place across the table at dinnertime. Tonight, though, there was no empty place. I felt like I was part of a family again, and that this house was becoming a home…a real home.

"Maybe we could watch a movie after dinner?" I didn't want this evening, this feeling, to end.

"I'd like to—but could we do it later? I have piano students coming at eight," Erin said.

"Sure. We could do it later. Or another night." I tried not to feel disappointed.

"It's so cool that you're a piano teacher." Devin took band at school and had always loved music.

"When did you learn to play?" I asked. From what Erin had told me so far, her childhood hadn't sounded like the type to include music lessons.

"It was a bit of a fluke, actually. When I was a kid there was a music teacher in the apartment next to ours. She gave me lessons and in exchange I looked after her dog when she went on weekend trips."

"Sweet deal," Devin said.

"Actually, Miss Prentice got fair value. She went on

a lot of weekend holidays. I've often wondered what my oh-so-correct piano teacher used to do on those weekends."

Erin winked at me, and I was embarrassed to find myself blushing in response. "Perhaps Miss Prentice was in the Secret Service," I said.

"Oh, no doubt. She was in secret service to someone, for sure."

The twins looked like they didn't know whether to laugh or pretend they didn't understand what Erin meant. In the end we all laughed, except for Shelley who turned in confusion from face to face, then went back to eating her pie.

"Would anyone like—" A muffled sound from the front of the house interrupted my offer of tea or coffee. "What was that?"

More noises were coming from the porch. First the sound of clunking footsteps, then the pounding of a fist on a door.

But not on our door. Erin's.

"Are you expect—"

Before I could finish the question, Erin was on her way out of the room. "I'm sorry," she said. "Can I leave Shelley here for a few minutes?"

I hurried after her, following her to the door. "Do

you think it's safe to go out there?" I checked through the window, but in the time it had taken us to eat our meal, the sun had gone down and it was too dark to see anything.

I hadn't yet turned on the porch light and I hesitated to suddenly do so now. I wasn't at all sure I wanted to alert this person to the fact that people were home in this half of the building.

"I have a good idea who this is," Erin said. "Don't worry. I won't be long."

She slipped outside before I could stop her. Immediately the person on the porch started swearing.

It was a man. And he sounded drunk.

I raced back to the kitchen. My daughters and Shelley were still sitting at the table, dessert forgotten in front of them.

"Mom, who's out there?" Devin looked like she was about to be sick, but I had no time to reassure her.

"I don't know." I locked the back door, thought for a second, then grabbed the phone.

"What should we do?" Jamie asked.

"Stay here," I ordered before heading back up the hall.

Through the closed door came the sound of muffled yelling. I opened it a crack and heard Erin say, "Here's sixty dollars. I don't have any more cash in the house."

"That's not enough, you bitch. She's your mother for God's sake."

"Don't remind me."

"Hey, you owe her."

"I don't owe either of you a damn thing."

"Yeah? That's not the way I see it."

"Well, I've already given you all I've got. What do you want me to do?"

The man's tone suddenly softened, turning oily and full of insinuation. "If you don't have money, you've got something else I'm interested in. You always have."

"God, Ritchie, you make me sick. Get out of here, you pig."

"Actually, you're too skinny to bother with now. What's the matter with you, anyway?"

Erin just swore at him.

"What did you say?" The man sounded outraged.

I heard the scuffling of feet. A dull thud. A loud moan.

Oh, no. I yanked the door open and burst outside. Brandishing the phone, I hollered, "I'm calling the police right now so you'd better start running."

"It's okay, Lauren." Erin calmly took the phone out of my hands and turned it off. "I'm fine."

It took me a moment to process the scene. Erin *was* fine, it was the man who'd taken a fall. Erin must have pushed him, because he was lying in a tangle at the bottom of the porch stairs.

As I watched he pulled himself up onto his elbows. He glared at me, a man about my age, surprisingly attractive despite his poor grooming.

"Who the hell are *you?*" he asked.

"None of your business," Erin said, answering for me.

I glanced from Erin to the man, then back again. "Are you sure we shouldn't call the police?"

"What do you think, Ritchie?"

Instead of replying, he swore. Then he made his way up to unsteady feet. After one more evil glare, he turned and started lumbering down the street.

"Screw you," Erin muttered after him. Her face was set in rebellious anger, but her trembling body revealed a more vulnerable reaction.

I put an arm over her slight shoulders. "Who *was* that?"

"My stepfather," Erin said in a monotone. "But I've always thought of him as Dad."

To my astonishment, once Ritchie was out of sight, Erin returned to the kitchen table and resumed eating her apple pie as if nothing had happened. Later, when Erin started to clear the plates, I stopped her.

"You've been through enough today. Go home and prepare for your students."

"Actually, this has been harder on you than on me. Believe me, I'm used to Ritchie. Besides, I can't leave you with this mess."

"You forget." I roped an arm around each of my daughters. "I own slaves."

"You're a stubborn broad, aren't you?" Erin threw up her hands. "Fine. I surrender. And Jamie and Devin? I owe you one, okay?"

An hour and a half later, the kitchen had been returned to order, the girls were in their rooms and I was relaxing in the living room when I heard a couple of taps at the front door.

Cautiously I moved into the foyer. Had that Ritchie character returned?

"Lauren? It's me."

I let Erin in. "What's going on? Did that man come back?" I gazed out through the murky lighting to the street.

"No, no, Ritchie's gone. I won't see him again for at least a month." Erin closed the door behind her. "Shelley's sleeping. I thought we should talk."

I gestured Erin into the living room. When Erin sat on one end of the sofa, I curled up on the other. "Is that man really your stepfather?"

"Unfortunately, yes. He married my mom when I was fourteen. I had a huge crush on him back then, if you can believe it."

"He's a good-looking man. And not that much older than you."

Erin nodded. "Yeah, my mom was practically a kid when she had me. She dated a lot while I was growing up, but Ritchie was her first steady guy. He used to flirt with me, and I just lapped it all up."

I hated knowing where this was headed. "Of course you did. Any young girl who'd grown up without a father would."

"You think?"

"Absolutely. There's no way you should blame yourself for what happened."

Erin smiled without mirth. "It's that obvious, huh?"

"I heard what he said to you on the porch." I couldn't hold myself back anymore. "Why did you give him your money? He's a disgusting criminal. You should press charges against him."

Erin shook her head.

"Why not?"

"Because it would kill my mother if something happened to him."

"They're still together?"

"Yeah."

"Does she know what he did?"

Erin didn't answer that. "We've had a rocky relationship my mom and I, but it all fell apart the year I got pregnant with Shelley."

Was I finally going to find out who the father was? But no, Erin skirted the subject again, focusing on her mother.

"Mom told me I was too screwed up to be a parent. And she sure as hell wasn't grandma material. That was the last time we spoke. Now Ritchie shows up every so often for a little pocket change and that's it."

Suddenly my own conservative, ultra protective mother didn't seem so bad. "Erin, you need to move on from these people. I don't see why you feel you have to give them your hard-earned money."

"It makes me feel better. I know it doesn't make sense. It's complicated, Lauren. Like a lot of things in my life."

She looked so sad. And beaten. I couldn't stand it. "But you've got so much going for you."

Again Erin shook her head.

"You do," I insisted. "You've got a great kid, a successful business, your own home…and friends."

I reached over to touch Erin's hand. It felt cold. "Don't let him get to you."

"Yeah. I know." Erin returned the squeeze with her fingers, then stood. "I should get home. I don't like leaving Shelley alone, even though there's just a wall between us."

I hated to see her leave. Erin looked so despondent. At the door, I couldn't resist giving her a hug. The thin woman felt fragile and stiff in my arms. "I'm glad I moved next door to you, Erin."

When she said nothing, I wondered if I'd embarrassed her. But when I stepped back, I saw tears in her eyes.

"Erin…"

The other woman held out a hand to stop me. She shook her head, then waited until she'd gathered her composure.

"That's nice of you to say," she finally replied. "I hope you still think that a year from now."

CHAPTER 8

As the weeks went by, I had less time to miss the people from my old life. My parents still weren't talking to me, and my phone calls from old friends had dwindled down to nothing.

Though they were nice women for the most part, we had run out of subjects to talk about. I didn't have the money to do the fancy Yorkville lunches, afternoons at the spa and shopping trips anymore. Nor did I have the luxury of devoting hours to charitable causes.

I had to work, or the girls and I would become one of those causes ourselves. And there was certainly no shortage of real, paying work to keep me busy. I'd followed through on my idea to distribute business cards at the country club and already a little business was dribbling our way from that.

When August ended, my mother took the twins to buy their school uniforms—a traditional outing that I had been afraid she would abandon this year.

She was still furious at me for moving to this part of the city. "I don't see why you won't let your father and me help you."

But help from my parents had too many strings attached, and so I continued to hope that they would eventually come around. Though expecting them to visit us on Carbon Road might always be beyond the realm of the possible.

Work at the agency was steady for all of September, and soon I was feeling more comfortable with my job. Erin and I still worked together the majority of the time, but I handled one or two new cases a week, and I continued to clean Adam's apartment twice a month, as well. I was out a lot, but between background checks and various administrative tasks, I usually spent at least one day a week behind a desk.

Then, the last week of September, Erin caught a bug and had to stay in bed for several days. Suddenly I found myself handling all the work at the agency on my own. I was surprised when I realized I could handle it…though I did turn down all offers of new business that week.

By month end, Erin declared herself back to normal, but I wasn't too sure. Erin had a lingering cough that worried me, but she refused to go get checked out.

"God, I hate this crap." Erin looked up from the stack of papers on her desk. She was inputting the hours from our manual logs into the computer, part of the month-end accounting that resulted in the production of invoices to mail to our clients.

"Really? I think this is kind of fun." I totaled a column of figures on the calculator with satisfaction. Another monthly bank statement all reconciled.

Erin had been behind six months when she'd first shown me the books. I was enjoying the accounting almost as much as I enjoyed the actual casework.

"Fun?"

"Sure. It helps me see the big picture as far as the business is concerned." The more I learned, the more impressed I became. This was a smartly run little operation.

Erin glanced around the cramped room. "One day I'd love to get a real office. Something funky on Queen Street, with Karmeli and Holloway P.I. etched on a glass window front. Can you see it?"

"While you're dreaming, add an assistant to the picture."

"Hm. I'm picturing Orlando Bloom, how about you?" Erin tossed a stack of papers to her desk. "I can't read these numbers. Maybe I need glasses."

"Let me try." I exchanged chairs with Erin. I hadn't worked with this accounting program before, but it didn't take me long to catch on.

Erin stood and stretched. "How about some coffee? I could run to Murphy's and get us some."

"Just a small cup for me. I want to sleep tonight." It would have been quicker for Erin to go next door and use my coffeemaker, but I knew better now than to make the suggestion. For some reason Erin believed that only Murphy's coffee would do.

"I'll be right back."

She sounded relieved to have an excuse to get out of the house. Clearly she really did dislike the administrative side of the business. But I hadn't been kidding when I'd said I enjoyed it. By the time Erin returned with our coffee, I was printing out the invoices.

"I'll stuff those into envelopes," Erin offered, setting down her cup and going to the supply cupboard.

I sampled the coffee. Lord, but it was stiff. "Say, Erin, why don't we schedule next week's work while we've got all the records out. Do you want that new client who called about his grandmother's ring?"

Erin had seemed intrigued by the case. The client was sure that his ex-wife had sold his grandmother's diamond ring and he wanted us to track it down for him.

"He wanted to meet on Tuesday afternoon, right? I can't make that. Can you?"

"No. Tuesday afternoons are out for me."

"Right. I forgot." That was why I had Ava's case because Adam had wanted a cleaner on Tuesday afternoons. At the time I'd assumed Erin had a conflict with another job. But when I'd gone through the logs, I hadn't seen any hours from Erin for that time.

I flipped through the appointment calendar. Erin had nothing noted on Tuesday afternoon. I looked expectantly at my friend, but Erin didn't say anything further. Instead, she gulped down coffee and stared out the window at the brick wall of the neighbor's house.

I couldn't help but worry, just looking at her. Erin had lost a few more pounds while she'd been sick, pounds she couldn't afford to lose. Murphy was concerned, too. He wouldn't say much to me, but I'd seen him arguing with Erin a few times.

Like me, he was probably trying to convince Erin to see a doctor. If Erin wasn't better by next week, maybe Murphy and I would try ganging up on her. Between the two of us, we might be able to make her listen.

The next week, Sherry Frampton, the banking VP with the cheating husband, called the office to let us know that she was going out of town on business again. I happened to be in the office, so Erin put the call on speakerphone.

"I want you to get some good footage of Martin this time," Sherry said. "You need to zoom right in on his face."

Erin was sitting back in her swivel chair, stocking feet on the desk. She'd been feeling better this week, though her cough was still lingering. "Sherry, we shot his license plate, the car, and got a good profile of him as well. It was Martin. No doubt about it."

"He could have lent his car to a friend. Or even his brother. They're practically twins."

Erin rolled her eyes at me, but when she spoke she gave no sign of being frustrated. "Okay, we'll give it another go. How long are you away?"

"Three nights, starting today. My flight leaves in two hours. And I'm willing to pay you to sit outside that house all three nights if that's what it takes to get absolute proof that he's screwing around."

"Will do. Call me when you get back." Erin hit the end button with her heel, then tipped the chair back even farther.

"Poor Sherry," I said. "She just can't believe it, can she?" Still, I thought she was smart to insist on the truth.

Nasty news was bad enough. Nasty surprises were the worst. Surely, if you saw the bad stuff coming, you'd be better prepared to handle it.

Like if I'd realized Gary was falling for his yoga instructor from the beginning, I would have been able to…

But even with hindsight I couldn't see what I could have done differently. Except, perhaps, move my family to the other side of the country. But even that drastic action would have been only a temporary fix.

"Do you want to work on this one together?" I asked.

"I was hoping you could handle it on your own."

I supposed I could. But in the past Erin and I had done the late-night surveillance jobs together. It was more fun that way.

"You've been working here for over two months

now. You're a pro," Erin said. "Just make sure you don't forget your coffee. It's a lot harder to stay awake when you're working all night on your own."

Later that night, I stopped in at Murphy's with my empty travel mug. I had stocked my car with everything I could imagine needing and I'd reread the surveillance chapter of my online P.I. course several times. I was as prepared as I could possibly be.

The diner was almost empty. Murphy seemed slightly on edge. I wondered if he'd had a bad day. But when I asked him, he just looked at me like my question made no sense.

Maybe all days were bad to Murphy.

"On assignment tonight?" he asked as he filled my cup.

"Yes. It's my first time going solo. I hope Erin knows what she's doing."

"Yeah, me, too," he muttered.

"What was that?" Why was he still on my case? Did he still think I wasn't going to be able to handle this job?

"Nothing." Murphy swabbed at the counter. "Your girls were in here the other day. Nice kids."

"Thanks. I hope you didn't serve them BLTs?"

He almost smiled. "Nah. I sent them to the smoothy-and-wrap place down the road. Figured that would be more their style."

It probably was. But why had Murphy cared?

Single moms and kids, I remembered Erin saying. They were Murphy's weakness. Yet, I was a single mom and Murphy didn't seem to like me too much. For the hundredth time I wondered what it was about me that rubbed him the wrong way.

And why I kept returning for more of his punishment.

I watched him slide out the filter holder from the machine, then dump the damp coffee grounds into the trash. I realized that I never saw him walking around the neighborhood, shopping or even visiting Erin. The only place I ever saw him was here, at the diner.

"You put in such long hours. Early mornings. Late nights. When do have time for yourself?"

Murphy arched his eyebrows. "I'm the boss. I make time when I need to."

The cryptic answer annoyed me. "So, if you wanted to take off on a Tuesday afternoon, for example, you would?"

His eyes narrowed. "Sure. Tony can handle the

place for a few hours." He leaned his head a little to the side. "Any particular reason you mentioned Tuesday?"

I studied his face carefully. "Any reason I shouldn't?"

His expression remained impassive. Yet, I had a feeling he knew what I was fishing for.

"Erin's busy on Tuesday. I thought she might be doing something with you."

"Doing something. As in a date?"

"Well…?"

"I'm not seeing Erin on Tuesday or any other day. Except here. The girl's addicted to coffee—what can I do?" Murphy glanced at his watch. "Don't you have a job tonight? I've got customers waiting for that stool."

I glanced around. The man who'd been sitting in the far corner when I'd come in was gone now. We were alone.

"Of course you do." I grabbed my coffee and left.

I didn't make it home until three in the morning. Martin had stayed out very late with his lady love. But at least I'd been rewarded for my vigilance. They'd indulged in a long, deep kiss on the landing, and the woman had even walked Martin to his car.

Apparently the late hour and the deserted street had made Sherry's boss overly confident. Hiding in the back seat of the Volvo, I had felt invisible. I'd parked in the shadows. Martin hadn't been so clever.

At home I left a note on the counter for the girls to make their own breakfast and lunch the next day. Then I fell into bed and slept until ten.

It was a good sleep. Deep and uninterrupted. The kind of sleep I'd had all the time before my marriage had unraveled.

When I woke up, it was too late to catch Erin at Murphy's. She'd be home again by now. Anxious to show Erin the footage I'd taken last night, I dressed quickly then ran next door.

Erin took a long time to answer. She looked as if she'd just rolled out of bed, too, but she'd obviously been at work for a while because she was holding a file in her hand.

"So? How'd it go last night?"

"Terrific. Wait till you see." I handed over the camera.

"It was kind of fun on my own, Erin. I had the

perfect cover story if one of the neighbors came out to complain or reported me to the police."

But no one had. I'd been so inconspicuous, it was like I was never there.

Erin opened the display window on the camera, then replayed the digital recording. She grinned when it was over. "Excellent stuff."

"Thanks. Do you want me to come in and we can work on the report together?"

"I think that can wait until later. You're meeting Ava this afternoon, aren't you?"

"That report's done. I have time to help you—"

"No need. Really." Erin started to close the door.

I put out a hand to stop her. "Are you sure you're okay?" I decided that she didn't look tired so much as unwell. Had the bug come back? "Have you eaten anything today?"

"I'm fine. Honestly. Just haven't had time to shower or put on any makeup yet."

"Okay…" I started to leave, then stopped. "Want to get together later tonight? I got a free DVD rental with my grocery purchase yesterday."

"Great. Let's do that."

I stood on the stoop as Erin all but shut the door in my face. Then I shrugged. I'd see how Erin was looking later tonight and if she still seemed bagged, I'd insist on taking her to the doctor myself.

At home, I printed out Ava's report, then cleaned the mess the girls had left in the kitchen that morning. At ten minutes to twelve, I went to meet Ava at Murphy's.

It had been windy last night, and the sidewalks were almost hidden beneath a layer of red and gold leaves. I hardly noticed the signs of the changing season, though, as I crossed the street and passed the hardware store.

Portly Nick Turchenko was sweeping the sidewalk outside the grocery store as I walked by.

"How's Iris?" I asked, stopping to chat for a few minutes. Over the past month I'd gotten to know the Turchenkos quite well, though I still had difficulty understanding them. The Turchenkos were Ukrainian and though they'd lived in Canada for a decade now, their accents were still as thick as their waistlines.

"Look at these pears." Nick pointed to a basket that was almost overflowing with golden Bartletts. "Your girls would love these pears."

Nick insisted on giving me a bag before he would allow me to carry on my way. Through the window of Murphy's Grill, I could see Ava sitting at her usual stool, waiting patiently.

I wondered how her campaign was going to woo the

eligible dentist. The last time I'd seen her she'd been excited about a little bit of progress. She and Adam had had coffee together after work that week. They'd talked about books and movies…everything had gone really well, she thought.

Maybe the two were now dating. With any luck Ava was meeting me this week to tell me that she no longer required my services. Though the money was nice, I hoped that this would be the case. I still felt weird snooping around Adam's condo as I cleaned. And I wanted more for Ava.

She looked up as I pushed through the diner door. She was wearing her usual blue uniform, and her red hair had been smoothed out into glossy waves. She looked pretty, but not very happy.

"How are things?" I asked, settling in next to her, my hopes fading.

"Not good." She stirred her coffee listlessly. "I thought we had such a good time the other week. But he never suggested we do it again."

"You haven't been seeing each other?"

"No."

I hesitated, then passed her the report. While she started to read, I automatically checked around for Murphy. He was behind the till, making change, apparently oblivious to my presence. As usual, my gaze lingered on him longer than I would have liked. Why I continued to find the man attractive, I couldn't say. I had to be careful or I would become as pathetic as Ava.

Murphy wandered up to us, coffeepot in hand. He gave Ava a refill, then tried to fill a mug for me.

"No coffee for me this afternoon," I said. I'd had two cups that morning but had taken no time to eat and my stomach was revolting.

"Then what do you want to order?" He hesitated. "You're not planning on sitting here and taking up one of my stools and not ordering anything?"

Oh, Lord, the man was stubborn. "Fine. I'll have a cup of coffee."

His smile was full of satisfaction. "That's what I thought. Here you go. It's on the house."

He turned and sauntered toward the kitchen.

"On the house?" I stared after him. "Then why in the world—" There really was no understanding Murphy, I decided.

Beside me, Ava had gone pale.

"Are you okay?"

She closed the report and then her eyes.

I knew she must have just read the paragraph in my

report where I'd described what I'd found in Adam's bathroom. This Tuesday there had been two tooth-brushes in the glass by his sink. I'd hoped the extra toothbrush might belong to Ava. But obviously not.

"Who is she?"

"According to the list of calls on his phone, I think she's J. Mallory." I prayed the name wouldn't ring any bells and it didn't seem to. It would have killed Ava to find out Adam was sleeping with another woman from their office.

"He hasn't been seeing her long." Ava swallowed hard. "It probably won't last."

"Oh, Ava… Maybe it's time to move on," I suggested gently.

"But we're perfect for each other. And I've invested so much into this relationship."

Yes, she had. She'd invested time, money and lots of heartbreak.

"It might be smart to cut your losses. He's dating someone else."

She shook her head. "I've got to give this one more try. Find out who J. Mallory is, Lauren. I've got to know."

I didn't see how that would help her. It would only bring her more pain. "There are lots of other guys."

"Not in my office. Not in my circle. Adam was

supposed to be *it*, Lauren. I can't just give up. Not until I know I did everything I possibly could."

Ava turned away as her lips quivered.

What else could I say without being cruel? "Ava, have you thought about going to a therapist?"

She shook her head. "I know what a therapist would say. The same thing you're saying. But Adam is so nice and he's gentle and funny. We belong together."

She looked at me and there was so much hurt and ache in her eyes that I could feel my own heart contract painfully in sympathy.

Clearly Ava needed something. And desperately.

I knew only one thing.

It wasn't Adam.

CHAPTER 9

The next Tuesday I woke up at the usual time to the sound of rain. I lingered in bed and thought about the new client Erin had asked me to meet.

This was the third time she'd asked me to cover for her on a Tuesday afternoon. I was glad to help her out. But my curiosity was mounting. Even when I asked directly, Erin wouldn't tell me why she was always busy at that time.

I knew I should respect her privacy and just leave it alone.

But with every week that passed, I became more convinced that she and Murphy were keeping something important from me. Either they didn't trust me or they didn't think I could handle the truth. Both possibilities were insulting.

I lazed in my bed another five minutes. The fact that it was raining was giving me an idea. The bad weather would give me an excuse to wear a trench coat today and carry an umbrella. Both would help mask my identity.

By the time I got out of bed, my mind was made up. As I piled turkey, lettuce and cheese inside bagels for the girls' lunches, I told myself not to feel guilty. I was Erin's partner. I had a right to know what was going on.

I still had in my mind the possibility that Erin was hooked on some sort of street drug. I could see why she wouldn't want to tell me. She'd pegged me as a "straight arrow" the first day she'd met me.

If she—and possibly Murphy, too—were involved in illegal activities, then I needed to find out and protect myself and my children.

After the girls left for school, I went to Murphy for coffee. It was part of my routine and to deviate from my routine would have invited questions. Still, I was worried that my guilt and anxiety would give me away, so I didn't say much. As I sat hunched over my coffee cup, listening to Erin and Murphy, I wondered if I was imagining the tense undercurrent to their banter.

Back at home I whiled away the morning with housework.

After lunch, I hid my distinctive blond hair in a bal-
lerina-style bun, then dug out an old pair of sunglasses
with huge, Jackie O. frames. I popped out the dark
glass—who wears sunglasses in the rain?—then slid
the frames onto my face and contemplated my reflection in the foyer mirror.

A good disguise, if I said so myself.

Now that I was prepared, I sat vigil in a chair over-
looking the street. Only twenty minutes later I saw
Erin leave her house and hurry off in the direction of
Dupont Street.

I slipped on my coat and grabbed my umbrella, then
waited until Erin had turned the corner before I let
myself outside. Despite the rain, the air was heavy and
warm and I immediately started to perspire.

Only maybe it wasn't the heat. Maybe it was my
nerves that were making me sweat.

Though I'd now worked on dozens of cases for Erin,
I'd never followed anyone before, certainly never
anyone I knew. I didn't feel like a private investigator.
I felt like an idiot.

Nevertheless, I stuck with the plan, crossing
Carbon Road and heading up a block to Dupont. In
the dull gray light, the old neighborhood looked more
dismal than usual. The neon sign in the window of

the tattoo parlor provided the only splash of color on the block.

The rain had pasted the last of the autumn leaves to the sidewalk, and I felt them mushy and slightly slippery under my feet. In my old neighborhood, the landscaping services would have finished bagging all the leaves for recycling. Lawns would be clipped and raked neatly for the winter months.

A nerve-splitting screech of airbrakes alerted me to a bus approaching from the west. A block ahead, Erin stood waiting at the stop. She wore an old denim jacket, with the collar pulled up around her neck. Thanks to the rain, her hair had frizzed to double its usual volume.

I waited until the last moment before stepping out from the hidden doorway and dashing for the open door. I boarded right behind Erin, and actually brushed against her shoulder as I walked past her to the back of the crowded bus.

My heart was pounding, I was certain my ears were burning a brilliant red, but Erin didn't even glance in my direction.

I clung to a metal pole and waited. At each stop more people piled on the bus; very few got off. The majority would probably connect with the subway at the Dupont stop. I had to assume that that was Erin's intention, too.

With people pressed in on all sides, I grew warmer. I longed to remove my coat, but of course I couldn't. Every now and then I lost sight of Erin and at each stop I scanned the backs of the people who spilled out to the street, not wanting to miss her.

As I'd guessed, at the Dupont station stop, Erin hit the street, only to disappear seconds later on the stairs down to the subway.

I pushed through the crowd, following as closely as the mob of people around me would allow. Even so, I was only just in time to see Erin choose the south-bound tunnel. I went that way, too, running a few paces to shorten the gap between us. Hearing an approaching train, Erin began to jog. So did I.

The subway pulled up to the platform and the doors opened. I jumped onboard the same car as Erin, but two doors down. Collapsing into a seat, I took a deep breath.

It seemed amazing to me that not once had Erin glanced in my direction. In fact, Erin seemed impervious to all of her surroundings this afternoon. Like many commuters, she was moving on autopilot, through a sequence of transfers that she had performed numerous times before.

The subway started moving and I felt my heart rate

speed up, too. We stopped at Spadina, St. George, Museum, Queen's Park. Each time, I twisted in my seat so I could scan the departing passengers.

Then it happened. Amid the crowd on the platform I spotted a tall woman with frizzy hair wearing a denim jacket. It was Erin.

"Excuse me!" I pushed through a group of teenagers. The back of my trench coat only just slipped free of the doors as they closed behind me.

I glanced around. Erin was already disappearing up the escalator to the street.

I hurried after her, hugging the left-hand side of the escalator, rushing past others who were content to travel at a slower pace. At the top of the escalator, I searched the crowds and again I was lucky, spotting Erin just before she disappeared into the tunnel that would lead to University Avenue.

Hidden in the crowds, I followed, my thoughts lost in the thundering of footsteps as they echoed on the concrete walls. I raced up the stairs to the street, wondering how much farther. Where would she go now that we had left the relative predictability of the public transit system?

It was still raining when I burst out on the street. I popped my umbrella and turned a full circle.

Thank goodness for Erin's hair. She stood out from a herd of pedestrians crossing the street toward Toronto General.

Again I ran, catching the light just before it changed. As I stepped up to the sidewalk, I let out a relieved breath. Then immediately panicked. Where had she gone?

I swung left, right. How could I have lost her?

The Toronto General Hospital was in front of me, occupying the entire city block. The twins had been born here. I remembered Gary—

Wait. There was Erin, headed for the College Street entrance.

I collapsed my umbrella and took off. My mind raced along, too, seeking possible reasons for Erin to be going to a hospital. Was this visit somehow connected to a case?

But Erin never billed her time on Tuesday afternoons. Of course, she could be working pro bono, but more likely this was a personal mission.

Maybe she was finally getting that cough checked out…but no. The way she'd been traveling, almost by autopilot, made me certain that this was a route she'd taken many times before.

Perhaps her mother was sick? Erin had said she was

a heavy drinker. Maybe she had health problems related to that. And Erin was embarrassed and hadn't wanted to admit it to me.

I yanked open the hospital door, dashed inside, then jerked to a stop. Erin stood just a few yards ahead of me. Her slender shoulders were slumped and her arms hung limply at her sides. She swayed slightly and I fought the impulse to step forward and steady her.

After the mad rush to get here, Erin seemed strangely devoid of purpose. Or maybe she was just gathering her strength for whatever lay ahead.

I wanted to put an arm around her, ask her if she needed help, but I couldn't blow my cover now.

When Erin resumed walking, so did I. Erin was moving purposefully again, and from the set of her shoulders, it was clear there was no pleasure at all in what lay before her.

I wasn't familiar with this part of the hospital. Both the Emergency Department and Maternity were on the other side of the building. I was really roasting now and longed to unbutton my coat. Instead, I pulled up the collar to hide as much of my face as possible in case Erin glanced back.

She didn't. In the next minute, Erin reached for a door and disappeared inside another room. I checked the sign posted on the wall and immediately felt that there had to be a mistake. This was the Immunodeficiency Clinic.

In other words…an AIDS clinic.

My mind went numb for a moment. Then it exploded as I raced through the possible reasons Erin would be going to an immunodeficiency clinic.

She could be here to help someone. An old friend. Her stepfather. Even her mother.

I pressed my back to the wall, knowing I could follow no farther. She'd see me for sure if I went in after her.

CHAPTER 10

I went for a long walk in the Legislative grounds, just a few blocks north of the hospital. My black shoes were soaked by the time I stopped for a coffee and a muffin.

The little treat was expensive, and my latte didn't taste as good as I'd expected. Murphy's coffee had obviously ruined my taste buds. I wondered if the damage was permanent.

Not that it really seemed to matter right then.

What had Erin been doing at that AIDS clinic? I wanted to believe she was there to support a friend or family member, but that rationalization required me to ignore a growing pile of evidence that pointed in quite another direction.

Finally, I had a theory that accounted for the facts.

Erin's excessive weight loss. Her lingering sickness and cough. Even the locked medicine cabinet.

As my numbness and disbelief wore off, questions mounted.

I didn't know a lot about HIV or AIDS, but I'd watched a few programs on TV—enough to know that the disease progressed in stages. Also, AIDS was no longer a guaranteed death sentence. Hopefully if Erin did have the disease, it was something she could control and live with for a very long time.

An hour and a half later, I felt calm enough to return to the hospital. As I made my way back, another piece of the puzzle fell into place.

Erin's illness would explain why she'd been so anxious to take on a new partner and why Murphy had been worried I wouldn't stick....

I couldn't fault either of them for that—only, when had Erin planned on telling me about this?

I retraced my steps into the hospital, only this time I continued through the door to the clinic. At the reception desk a kind-looking woman gave me a smile.

"Can I help you, miss?" she asked in a Jamaican accent.

"Thank you. I'm a friend of Erin Karmeli's." On impulse I took a pamphlet from the desk and folded it into my pocket. "Is she still here? I was supposed to meet her."

The smile faded as the receptionist checked her records. "I'm afraid you're too late. She finished with Dr. Channing half an hour ago. She's probably done her blood work by now, too."

"Oh, dear. That's too bad."

The receptionist said nothing, but I could guess what she was thinking. What kind of friend showed up late at a time like this?

The kind who didn't know the other friend was sick, that's what kind.

I turned away from the desk and started walking. Fast. If only I could understand why Erin hadn't told me the truth about her Tuesday appointments. Did she think I would judge her?

Probably. People did judge about HIV, didn't they, just as they judged about other sexually transmitted diseases. You assumed a person had to be a drug user or promiscuous.

Of course, Erin had admitted to being both of these in her life before Shelley.

Oh my God—Shelley. Could she have the virus? Had Erin been infected when she was pregnant?

I felt something wet on my face and realized that I

was outside again and it was still raining. I stared at the street in front of me without really seeing it.

How sick *was* Erin? What was her treatment plan? What were her options?

All these questions were making me insane. I had to talk to someone. As soon as possible. I checked my watch. Erin was probably picking up Shelley from school right now. There'd be no chance for the two of us to speak privately until after Shelley was in bed.

I needed to do something *now*.

I thought about Murphy. I was sure he knew about the HIV. But would he talk to me? I sincerely doubted my ability to charm or coerce any information out of him if he decided not to cooperate.

Which left… What? Did I have any other options?

I was supposed to be a private eye, I reminded myself. I ought to be able to think of something.

And that's when I had my brilliant idea. I would talk to Erin's doctor.

At 5:35 p.m. a brown-haired man with gray at his temples entered the parking arcade and headed in my direction. I was leaning against a silver BMW parked in a stall with a small sign indicating that this spot was reserved for B. L. Channing, M.D. I'd been waiting for a couple hours now, during which time I'd seen many men come and go from the arcade.

But my instincts told me that this was the one.

The man looked to be in his late forties or maybe fifty, in other words just a little older than me. He was medium height, slender and he wore his unbuttoned trench coat, gray pants and striped shirt with a sense of style I did not expect from a doctor.

But it was his face that drew my attention most.

The man looked so weary. Not just tired from a long day at work, but absolutely weary as if he'd been carrying a burden for a long time.

I continued to wait as he moved toward me. He stopped cold when he was about ten feet away. His expression reflected mild surprise, curiosity…and something else. Appreciation?

Earlier I'd taken my hair out of the bun, tossed the sunglass frames and removed my coat so that I could lean against it and protect myself from the light film of dust on his vehicle. Now I straightened and folded the coat over my arm.

"Dr. Channing?"

He tilted his head slightly to one side. "Yes?"

"I'm Lauren Holloway. I've been waiting to speak with you."

His gaze shifted to the imprint of my coat on his car. "I see that."

I held out my hand, hoping good manners would keep him talking long enough for me to engage him. I was right. He accepted my hand and introduced himself.

"Burke Channing." He cocked his head again. "We haven't met before, have we?"

I considered pulling out my P.I. license and telling him I was working on a case. But I wasn't that good of an actor. "No, we haven't. I'm here because of a friend of mine. Her name is Erin Karmeli."

His gaze dropped from my face, to my pearls, to the blue sweater set I'd put on that morning. "You're a friend of Erin's?"

Though his tone was polite, there was no mistaking the incredulity behind the question.

"We're next-door neighbors. And business partners." And, yes, damn it, we were friends, too. I took a deep breath, determined to stay on my best, most professional behavior. "You remember Erin, right? She's one of your patients."

"I have no trouble recalling the names of my patients."

He tried to step by me, but I moved in front of the

driver-side door. His answer had been clever, neither confirming nor denying that Erin was indeed his patient. But I already knew that she was.

"She's HIV-positive, isn't she? She hasn't told me, her Tuesday afternoon appointments have been a big secret, but today I followed her, and now I know."

I realized I was talking too loud, too fast, and I didn't care. I'd known something was wrong with Erin almost from the start. Why hadn't it occurred to me that it might be an illness?

Oh my God, I knew someone with HIV.

AIDS wasn't part of my life. It belonged on TV, in dark alleys…in Africa.

But then, until a year ago, divorce hadn't been a part of my life, either. Nor had semidetached homes, blue-collar neighborhoods and greasy-spoon diners.

Suddenly it was all too much. I covered my mouth, embarrassed to realize I was *crying*—actually sobbing— in a parkade in front of a man I didn't know.

"I'm sorry." I struggled for control. "I know about patient confidentiality and all that stuff. But I really need you to tell me that Erin is going to be okay. She will be, right?" I gulped for air. "I mean there are drug cocktails and treatments and I *know* there isn't a cure, but she's still going to live for a very long time…."

Dr. Burke Channing laid a hand on my arm. He had a soft touch and his gray eyes were kind.

"You're in shock," he said. "Take a deep breath."

I did.

"And another."

A tremor passed over me and he patted my back gently. "You need to go home and talk to Erin. Tell her what you think and give her a chance to confide in you."

He spoke as if he cared and I decided I liked Erin's doctor very much.

"She's my best friend. Pretty much my only friend. She can't die."

Burke Channing looked torn. Finally he said, "You seem like someone who would have lots of friends."

Funny he should say that. Because once I had. I'd had so many friends I'd had trouble scheduling all the lunches and tennis games and charity meetings into my calendar.

"A lot of things changed after my divorce."

An understanding sort of look crossed over his face. He said nothing for a while, then asked, "When did that happen?"

"Over a year ago." I looked at my hands, twisted in front of me. These were the same hands that had once been linked with Gary's. He'd slipped an engagement ring on that finger. A wedding band six months later.

"My wife died last November."

I was startled when he said that. He just didn't seem like the sort of man who would tell a strange woman that sort of information.

Then I remembered my first impression of him and I gave him a closer look. I saw that the burden he was weighed down with wasn't fatigue. It was grief.

"It's hard being alone again, isn't it?" I said. "Did you have children?"

"Unfortunately, no. You?"

"Twin girls. They're fifteen." I checked my watch and grimaced. "They'll be wondering where I am. Actually where *dinner* is, more specifically."

I dabbed tears away with my fingers, until he passed me a tissue. "Thanks."

"Can I walk you to your car?" he offered.

"I took the subway." I backed up, suddenly astounded and embarrassed that I'd come to a stranger for answers about Erin. All things considered, Burke Channing had taken my ambush very well.

"Let me give you a ride home."

"I'm sure it's out of your way. I live in Dovercourt Village."

His brows went up and he looked at my pearls again. The Cartier watch on my wrist.

I shrugged. "We had to move after the divorce."

"I'm sorry."

"So am I, for disturbing you this way. I'll talk to Erin as you suggested." I headed for the exit, but he called me back.

"Lauren? The offer for a ride still stands. I'm always looking for an excuse to put off the moment I go into that empty house."

He pulled a phone from the breast pocket of his jacket. "Call your children and let them know where you are and who you're with. I promise I'm harmless."

And then he smiled, and I felt the effect right down to my sodden toes. I wiggled them in my ruined black leather shoes and thought how lovely it would be not to have to walk all the way to the subway, then take the transfer to the bus, then walk to my house.

Besides, I would get a chance to talk some more with Burke.

"Thank you. I'd love that."

From the dry warmth of Burke's car, I used his cell phone to call home. My fingers trembled a little as I punched in the numbers. I still wasn't myself. I lifted the phone to my ear. It smelled slightly of a very delicious men's cologne.

At home my phone rang four times then the machine kicked in. Belatedly I recalled that Jamie was working late tonight and Devin had asked to sleep over at a friend's.

I left a brief message, then closed the phone and handed it back to Burke. We weren't going anywhere fast. Not at this time of day. I probably would have arrived home faster by transit, but I didn't regret my decision.

This was so nice. I felt comfortable with Burke Channing and I realized that it was because he was the type of person I had hung out with all the time in my old life. The type of person I did not meet out on the street at Carbon Road or in the shops along Dupont Street.

I wondered how far I was taking him out of his way, and if he really didn't mind giving me a lift. "Where do you live?"

"Yonge and Lawrence."

I could picture his neighborhood immediately. A mix of homes and town houses, not as affluent as Rosedale, but definitely upscale. "Is it the same house you lived in with your wife?"

"Yes, Stephanie and I moved in five years ago. She

loved that house, but it's too big for one person. I know I should sell it and I will. Soon."

"I've read that it's a mistake to make major changes in your life until more than a year after you've lost a loved one."

"*You* moved," he noted.

"I put it off for as long as I could. I thought the girls had had enough upheaval in their lives. But our financial situation was too tight for me to avoid reality forever."

"Want to tell me what happened?"

To my surprise, I did. I gave him a shorter version of the story than I'd shared with Erin and it seemed to come out easier the second time around.

"So where is Gary now?" Burke asked when I was through.

"He and his yoga babe are in Chennai, India, last we heard."

"You're kidding."

"He's studying yoga at some famous center there. Krishnam-something-or-other."

Burke shook his head. "The guy must have been crazy to leave someone like you. And two daughters, as well." He shook his head again. "Most men want to have sons, but I always wanted a daughter."

He could have been feeding me a line, but I didn't think so. As well as being kind, there was something very genuine and honest about Burke Channing. Besides, I had a feeling that eligible male doctors probably didn't need to pick up their women from a parking arcade.

"Down this street," I directed, once we approached my neighborhood. Burke drove past the tattoo parlor, the hardware store, the diner....

Murphy. I made a mental note to talk to that man and give him a piece of my mind. I could almost understand why Erin had felt she needed to keep this secret. But after all this time, Murphy should have trusted me with the truth.

Burke took the corner and I leaned forward in my seat. "That's our house. Twelve A, Carbon Road."

I tried not to think about how it must look to him. The shabby house's flaws were all too visible to me right now. But Burke wasn't looking at the house.

He parked, then turned to face me. "I'm not sure if this is appropriate, but I'd like to see you again."

For a while I'd almost forgotten that he was Erin's doctor. I wanted to see him again, too, but the situation was complicated.

"I need to talk to Erin first."

"I understand." He opened the glove compartment

and pulled out a card. "Call me if you have questions after that."

"Will you talk to me? About Erin?"

"If she's okay with it."

"I'm not sure she will be."

"Call me anyway."

I didn't answer, just thanked him for the ride, then turned to face the twin houses in front of me. The drive home with Burke had provided a distraction, but now the weight of what I'd discovered that afternoon settled back on my shoulders.

And seemed just as unbelievable.

Erin couldn't be HIV-positive.

Yet, she was.

I heard Burke's car pull away from the curb, but I didn't turn to look. Erin's car wasn't parked out front, so she was probably on a job. Still, I couldn't resist going to her door and knocking.

Almost at once I heard footsteps from inside, and my heart began to thud. It seemed as if Erin was home after all. What in the world was I going to say to her? One look at my face and Erin would know that her secret was out.

But it wasn't Erin who opened the door.

It was Murphy.

CHAPTER 11

Murphy answered the door sporting his usual two-day growth and wearing his plaid shirt and jeans uniform. Up close like this, without a counter dividing us, he seemed taller and more broad-shouldered than ever. His only reaction to my appearance on Erin's doorstep was a tiny twitch at the corner of his mouth. He couldn't have looked more impassive. Or more masculine.

Except for the Barbie doll in his hand.

"Should she be wearing white? It's after Labor Day, you know."

"Smart-ass." Murphy waved me inside.

The house smelled of Italian spices and rising bread. I guessed a pizza was baking in the oven. Shelley sat on the sofa, a pile of dolls and colorful outfits in her lap.

"Hi, Shell." I gave her a hug. "Where's your mom?"

"Working," Murphy and Shelley replied together.

"Where are the twins?" Murphy asked in turn and when I explained that they wouldn't be home until later, he asked if I wanted a glass of wine.

I did. I really did.

I followed him to the kitchen. "When will Erin be back?"

"Late." His back was to me as he poured from a half-full bottle on the counter.

"I take it this isn't business? We had nothing booked for tonight."

He shrugged. Either he didn't know where Erin was or he wasn't prepared to tell me. As I sank into a chair, I took stock of the room. A bowl, sticky with remnants of dough, sat next to the stove. A portion of the counter was dusted with flour and a rolling pin jutted out from the sink.

Apparently Murphy had made the pizza from scratch.

He handed me the glass of wine, then sat down opposite me. "Why were your shoes so wet?"

Under the table, I crossed my stockinged feet. I'd taken off my sodden shoes at the door. "In case you haven't noticed, it's raining outside."

"Your shoes were soaked. There's no standing water on the sidewalks."

"Who's the detective here? You or me?"

"What makes you think I'm playing detective? You got something to hide?"

Good Lord, the man was relentless. "Could you shut up for a moment and let me enjoy my wine?" If I'd ever needed a drink, today was the day. I took a sip of the chardonnay, then a long swallow. It helped, but not much.

Murphy leaned back in his chair and crossed his arms over his chest. With narrowed eyes he watched as I drank my wine, stealing most, if not all, of my enjoyment in the process.

I set my glass on the table. "I followed Erin to the clinic today."

Murphy lurched forward. "What?" His gaze shot to the hallway and he got up to close the door.

More quietly, I repeated myself. "I followed Erin to the Immunodeficiency Clinic today."

"Why the hell did you do that?"

"Neither one of you would tell me what was going on."

"What makes you think that I—"

"You knew, Murphy. Of course, you knew."

He glanced away, providing a confirmation that I hadn't needed. I could remember walking into the diner on several occasions to find him and Erin deep in private conversation. They'd always looked a little guilty when they'd realized I had seen them. At least now I knew what they had been talking about.

"Erin was planning to tell you."

"Really? When? In her will?"

The minute the ugly words were out I regretted them. "I'm sorry. That was terrible. But why *didn't* you guys tell me?"

It hurt that they hadn't trusted me. It hurt a lot.

He studied my face a few more seconds, and the grim lines around his mouth tightened. "She has AIDS, Lauren. Not cancer. Nice people don't get AIDS."

"So she thought I would judge her."

"Haven't you, already?"

I didn't know what to say. From the first moment I'd met Erin, I had judged her. At different times I'd thought she might be a drug abuser, a prostitute, an alcoholic. But none of that had prevented me from liking her.

"She was scared, Lauren."

"She still should have told me. We're next-door

neighbors and business partners." I closed my eyes for a moment. "And I thought we were friends, as well."

"Good. I'm glad to hear you say that. Erin could use an extra friend or two right now."

I figured Murphy was right. A support system had to be crucial for someone with a terrible, chronic illness. But Erin's circle was small and tight as far as I knew. In fact, Murphy might well be her closest friend.

"How long have you known?" I asked.

"Only about three months. And for your information, she didn't tell me, either. I guessed."

"I can't believe I didn't. The signs are so obvious now that I know what to look for."

"Yeah, she's really gone downhill these past few months."

I hated to hear him confirm my fears.

He went to the sink and started washing dishes. "What do you know about AIDS?"

"Just the basics, I guess. The virus attacks a person's immune system."

He added hot water, then turned to face me again. "That's right. And when the immune system is sufficiently weakened, the patient becomes susceptible to all sorts of infections."

"Is—is Erin's system quite weakened?"

"When T-cell counts dip below two hundred, a patient is considered to have full-blown AIDS. Erin's T-cell count has been below one hundred for over a year."

I let my head sink into my arms on the table.

"Lately Erin's been battling one infection after another. She simply has no ability to fight anything, anymore."

"But she could still live a long time, right?" I wanted so desperately for him to tell me that Erin wasn't going to die. Even if it was a lie. Just for a while, I wanted to hope.

"You believe what you need to believe, Lauren. That's what I tell Erin, too."

In other words, there was no medical hope. Murphy was talking about miracles.

"I hate this, Murphy. It's just bloody unfair. Erin's had such a hard life. You'd think she'd deserve a break. Especially after all she's done to turn her life around."

"I know."

"She runs her own business and she's a terrific mother. This shouldn't be her fate."

"Fate has never been known for kindness, Lauren. At least not in this neighborhood."

I snorted. "Not in the neighborhood where I come from, either."

For a year I'd railed on the injustice of being deserted by a man I'd loved and trusted. None of my friends had understood, or been as supportive as Erin had in the short time I'd known her. "She's one of the best friends I've ever had."

"Me, too."

I'd known the relationship between Murphy and Erin was close, but I couldn't believe Murphy would open up enough to admit it.

And then I saw the situation from another perspective. Not mine. But his. Erin had been a big part of his life for a long time. This had to be brutal for him.

"I'm sorry. I've been making this my pity party, not even thinking about how rotten you must feel."

He blinked, then turned away.

"You really love her, don't you?"

He kept his back to me as he answered. "She grows on a person."

Typical Murphy understatement. I couldn't imagine him ever telling a woman that he loved her.

"I met her doctor today. I was hoping he could give me a better idea of what Erin is facing."

"Is that who gave you the ride home?"

"How did you guess?"

"I saw the M.D. plates on his car."

I'd had no idea he'd noticed us drive up. "You *are* a detective, aren't you?"

"Not as good as you, apparently. I thought physicians were restricted by patient confidentiality. Not where pretty blondes are concerned, I guess."

What was his issue? Erin's privacy? And did he really think I was a pretty blonde?

"Don't worry. Dr. Channing didn't divulge any information that he shouldn't have."

Murphy gave me a look that radiated skepticism, but before either one of us could add anything else, the buzzer on the stove went off. He slipped on an oven mitt, then pulled the pizza from the oven. It looked delicious.

With perfect timing, Shelley burst into the room.

"Is it ready?" she asked, holding two of her dolls, both dressed in evening gowns.

Shelley.

I couldn't believe I'd forgotten to ask Murphy the most important question of all. I looked at him in alarm and he seemed to understand what I was thinking. He shook his head quickly, then mouthed, "She's fine."

I sank back into my chair with relief.

Then polished off the rest of my wine with one long swallow.

* * *

Murphy invited me to stay for pizza and since my girls were both out, I accepted. It was interesting to see how connected Murphy and Shelley were. That little girl really drew him out. At times he even smiled at *me*.

After dinner, we played Barbies—all three of us— until I heard Jamie arrive home. As I said goodbye to Murphy, I tried once more to get him to tell me where Erin was, but he remained closemouthed.

Back home I made my daughter an egg-white omelet, then sat at the table with her and chatted while she ate. Various chores kept me occupied for a few hours after that. I kept an ear out for Erin's return, but by eleven o'clock I finally gave up. My talk with Erin would have to wait until the next day.

But when I awoke, I discovered I had missed her again. She'd left a manila envelope under my door. "Shelley and I are going away for a few days. See you Friday."

Included in the envelope was a batch of background-check requests that the country club—our newest client—had sent by courier the previous day. I tossed them on the table in what had started out being our dining room, but was rapidly becoming my office.

I read Erin's note again, scowled, then crumpled the paper in my hands.

The next few days passed slowly. I worked from home on the background checks and other administrative tasks. My only respite was breakfast and coffee every morning at Murphy's. For inexplicable reasons, both Jamie and Devin had scorned the wrap-and-smoothy joint down the road and decided they loved hanging out at Murphy's. He spoiled them by preparing a whites-only omelet for Devin and giving Jamie fruit salad rather than bacon.

When I expressed interest in the same substitutions, however, Murphy practically snapped at me.

"Forget it." He dropped a plate in front of me, his regular breakfast special. "Like I said, I don't do custom orders."

Devin and Jamie both beamed, and I had to hide my amusement at their obvious delight. As he passed by the counter on the way to the kitchen, Murphy caught my eye and winked.... At least I *thought* he winked, but maybe I was wrong, because that would imply a sense of humor and Murphy seemed quite deficient in that department.

By Friday morning, I was desperate to see Erin, but the Toyota was still missing and all was quiet next door as I set out for the day.

I'd caught up with all the office work and had set

up a meeting with a prospective new client at Murphy's. I'd finally realized why Erin liked doing business at the diner. The atmosphere was loose and people could relax there. Murphy's aloof attitude allowed clients to ignore him and focus on the business at hand.

The meeting went well and I headed for the bank an hour later with a signed contract and a healthy retainer. When I arrived home a few minutes before the girls would be back from school, the message light on the phone was flashing. I expected the call to be from one of my daughters, or better yet, Erin, so I was surprised to hear a male voice on the recording.

"This is Burke Channing calling for Lauren Holloway...."

I listened in disbelief to the rest of his message. Erin's doctor wanted to take me out to dinner. Tonight. He'd left a number for me to call, but I'd been so dazed, I hadn't even attempted to write it down.

I replayed the message, this time with pen and paper in hand, then I erased it and sat, stunned, at the kitchen table.

I didn't know what to make of this, how to feel. A part of me was numb. Another part excited. Mostly, though, I was scared.

Burke had made it perfectly clear his call had nothing to do with Erin. He wanted a date. A real date. With me.

But I hadn't gone out with a man since I'd separated from Gary. I hadn't actually dated in more than eighteen years. The prospect was terrifying.

And yet...

A part of me wanted to go. Burke Channing was attractive, successful, and best of all, he seemed genuinely kind. Like me, he'd experienced a loss and was looking to make a new life for himself.

But he was also Erin's doctor. How would she feel about me dating him?

"Damn," I muttered, going to the front window to check for Erin's car, yet again. Nothing. How could Erin do this to me? Disappear without leaving any way for me to contact her. What if there was an emergency with the business? She hadn't even asked me to collect her mail....

I had, of course. I had the key to her house, as well as to the office and the business filing cabinet, so I'd let myself in every day. I'd sorted her mail neatly on the kitchen table. Business letters in one pile, junk mail in another. I'd also checked the answering machine in Erin's office and dealt with all the calls pertaining to business.

New clients continued to trickle in all the time,

most of them via the contacts that Erin had been introducing me to over the past few weeks, but some from my tentative networking efforts as well. Creative Investigations was more than just viable. It was downright successful. And I was only just realizing how lucky I was to be working there.

Fifteen minutes after I had last checked, I went to the window again. This time I saw Jamie walking briskly toward our house. Following at a distance of about ten yards was Devin. Before I could get to the door to open it for them, the phone rang.

I dashed back to the kitchen and picked up the receiver.

"Hello?" This time it *had* to be Erin.

But it was Burke. "Hi there, Lauren. How are you?"

The girls stormed the kitchen then. Jamie opened the fridge door while Devin went straight to the cookie cupboard. I turned my back to them.

"Mom, can I go to a party tonight?" Jamie asked, ignoring the fact that I was on the phone.

"Me and Denise want to see a movie," Devin added.

I gestured at them to be quiet, then covered my free ear with my hand.

"…that is if you like Vietnamese food," Burke concluded. "Would you rather have something else?"

"I'd like anything but Indian." Oh, God, Jamie was rolling her eyes. She'd totally gotten that jab at her father. I spoke quickly to cover up my slip, "Actually the Vietnamese sounds fine."

Wait a minute. Had I just accepted the date?

"Great. I'll pick you up at seven."

Yes. I had.

Darn it, Erin. Where the heck are you?

Despite their evening plans, Devin and Jamie arranged to still be at home when Burke arrived. I think they were curious and maybe a little protective of me. I expected introductions to be awkward, the girls to be resentful, sullen, maybe even angry. In their eyes, this man was a potential substitute in my life for their father.

But the twins were surprisingly docile. Even pleasant. And Burke struck the perfect note with them, expressing interest and asking questions without giving the impression of trying too hard.

"So what movie are you going to?" he asked Devin.

He was in jeans tonight, and his V-necked cashmere sweater revealed the neckline of a white T-shirt. He had safely straddled the line between casual and so-phisticated and I hoped I had, too, with my black pants and silk wraparound sweater.

Devin had the entertainment section of the paper spread out over the coffee table. "My friend and I like horror."

Burke leaned over the listings, then pointed. "One of my patients said this was good."

Jamie glanced over his shoulder. "Yeah, I've heard it's totally creepy."

I shuddered. "I don't know why you girls enjoy scaring yourselves to death." I picked out a jacket from the closet. Before I could put it on, Burke was there, helping me slip my arm into the sleeve. I caught a faint whiff of the cologne that had been on his cell phone and felt a little shiver pass over me.

The man looked, sounded and smelled delicious.

It didn't seem possible that he was really standing in the middle of my Carbon Road semidetached home, about to take me out for the evening.

Was this a sign that my luck was changing?

But then I thought of Erin, and knew that the answer was no.

Burke was easy to talk to. *Too* easy to talk to.

"Did you grow up in Toronto?" he asked, once our drinks had been served.

"I did."

"Rosedale?"

"How did you guess?" I folded the edge of the napkin in front of me, the first step in making the swans I used for my formal place settings.

"Takes one to know one. Here's another guess... your childhood was basically happy."

"Yes. Pretty much, it was. I did well at school, had lots of friends and a good, stable home. Dad worked in the financial district and Mom stayed home and doted on me. She raised me to do the same and was pretty devastated when Gary and I broke up. Almost more than I was."

"Must be hard as a parent, to see your child suffer. Even a grown child with children of their own."

"That wasn't it. I'm not sure she even thought about how I was feeling. She just saw me as a failure and my life as ruined."

"That's pretty harsh."

"I felt the same way, at times," I admitted. "I'd never pictured living my life as anything but married. But when it all fell apart, at least I knew better than to move in with my parents. That really would have killed me."

"Is that what your mother wanted you to do?"

I nodded. "She still does. She hasn't spoken to me

since I sold the house and moved to Carbon Road, though she's called the girls a few times. I think she's waiting for me to break."

"And will you?"

He had a small smile as he asked this, and I smiled, too. "I don't think so. That's one thing I've learned since my divorce. I'm stronger than I thought I was."

As the server arrived to take my plate, I realized that I'd talked all the way through the main course. I'd barely noticed anything I'd eaten.

"Have I been whining? I have, haven't I? I'm so sorry, I hate complainers."

Burke reached over to touch my hand. "You haven't been complaining. Not at all. Anyway, listening to you is infinitely better to what's going on in my own head."

"Why do you say that?"

"Since Steph died, I've been steeped in self-pity," he said matter-of-factly. "And I don't want to go there, tonight. I'd much rather talk a—"

A look of surprise, then concern crossed his face as he focused on something behind my right shoulder. I turned to see what the problem was.

Only to find Erin pulling up a chair to join us.

"Seems we've taken to following each other lately," she said to me.

Was it just my new knowledge, or did Erin's face look especially gaunt? Even in the dim lighting, there were dark smudges under her eyes. Her frizzy hair was pulled back in a ponytail and she was wearing tight jeans and a scoop-necked top that made it impossible not to focus, at least briefly, on her breasts.

"How could you have followed me tonight?" I asked. "You weren't home."

"I drove up just when you were getting into the good doctor's car. How's that for excellent timing? And speaking of my doctor...hello, Dr. Channing. This is quite a coincidence finding the two of you together."

Despite her casual tone, it was clear that Erin was really ticked off. Burke smoothed a hand down the front of his sweater, and pushed back on his chair slightly. "Erin, this isn't what you think."

"Oh?" Erin turned to me.

"Erin, I'm sorry. I wanted to talk to you before I accepted Burke's invitation to dinner, but of course I couldn't since you haven't been home for days. Where have you been?"

"Regrouping. Trying to get over the shock of being followed by someone I thought I could trust."

The food I'd eaten without noticing suddenly made

its presence very obvious. I put a hand to my gurgling stomach. "You saw me?"

"From the moment you got on the bus at Dupont. You need a refresher on that surveillance chapter, honey." Her gaze swung to Burke. "And what about you? Don't I have a right to my privacy?"

"Erin, I assure you I haven't spoken about your case with Lauren."

"You really expect me to believe that?"

"I asked Lauren to dinner because I found her attractive. We had certain things in common and I wanted to get to know her better. I hope that's why she accepted."

Erin pushed herself out of her chair. "Whatever."

"Erin—" I reached out a hand. "Don't go. We need to talk...."

But Erin was already gone.

CHAPTER 12

The date, which had started out much better than expected, crashed and burned at that point. We didn't have tea or coffee, just drove home after paying the bill. As Burke walked me to the front door, he didn't say a word about seeing me again.

I was glad. I felt too numb to talk.

Yes, I'd been wrong to follow Erin. Yes, it had been an invasion of privacy. But that misdemeanor paled in comparison with the larger issue before us.

As soon as Burke drove away, I headed downstairs to Gary's wine collection and selected a bottle of burgundy. It was just past nine o'clock. My kids had three hours until curfew.

I stepped outside again into the cold, gray autumn night. The air was still musty from a week of rain and the grass was spongy under my shoes as I hopped the hedge and walked across the lawn.

All the lights were out in Erin's half of the house, except for the back room on the second story. Erin's office. I went through the side-yard gate, then across the wooden deck to the kitchen door.

I tried it and found it locked. I didn't want to risk waking Shelley by knocking. But of course I didn't need to knock…I had a key.

As I let myself in, I felt what was becoming a very familiar attack of the guilts. *And Erin had thought being followed was bad.* Never mind. I had to do what I had to do.

Inside, a night-light in the hall allowed me to make my way through the kitchen to the stairs without stumbling on anything. To me it seemed as if my every step sent out squeaks of protest from the old oak floorboards.

Upstairs, I followed the hall to the closed door of Erin's office. I knocked softly. "Erin?"

A muffled curse sounded from the other side. A moment later the door swung open. "What the h—"

I lifted the wine bottle. "I brought refreshments." I searched the pocket of my jacket and pulled out a corkscrew.

Erin was in pajamas with thick socks on her feet. She'd used one of them to kick open the door without rising from her perch in the cushioned office chair. Now she rolled the chair back to her desk. I glanced at the illuminated computer screen in front of her.

Erin was working on a Word document; it looked like something technical and legal, like a contract. But before I could read the title at the top of the toolbar, Erin grabbed the mouse and closed the window.

The screensaver popped into view. It was a picture of Shelley as a toddler picking an apple from a tree.

"I'm sorry to barge in on you, Erin, but we need to talk." I went to the cupboard where she kept some glasses. I opened the wine, then filled the glasses and passed Erin one.

Though she didn't look pleased about the situation, Erin took a long swallow. I sat in the empty chair and sampled the wine. Like the dinner I'd eaten earlier, though, I couldn't taste a thing. I was trying not to stare at Erin too much, but it was difficult. Now that I knew the truth, the signs of her illness were so obvious.

Oh, Erin, poor Erin.

"You weren't supposed to know yet."

"Why?"

"What do you think? I didn't want to scare you off."

She'd needed a business partner. And she'd been afraid I would run if I knew about her illness. "Oh, Erin. You idiot."

I put down my glass then went to my friend with open arms. The hug was awkward with Erin in a chair and me standing. Still, as I pulled away, Erin gave me a rueful smile.

"You never fail to surprise me."

"Likewise."

We both laughed.

"So now you know I have AIDS—"

The words sounded so stark when spoken out loud. I swallowed, then waited for Erin to finish.

"—but I'm still not sure how you tracked down my doctor?"

"It was easier than you'd think. The receptionist at the clinic let his name slip into our conversation. I searched the hospital parkade until I found his reserved spot. Then I waited."

Erin looked impressed. "Good footwork."

"Yeah, but it didn't get me anywhere. As Burke already told you, he refused to discuss your situation with me."

"Burke?" Erin mimicked my use of his first name, her tone provocative.

I didn't rise to the bait. "He offered me a ride home and we talked. I found out he'd lost his wife to cancer last year, which gave us something in common. Not that Gary died, but he's almost as gone as if he had."

"Yeah, I remember hearing about Channing's wife. That happened just before Christmas last year. So what's going on with you two? Are you really dating?"

"It was just dinner. I probably won't see him again. Anyway, that isn't important. I want to talk about you. How did this happen?"

Erin seemed less comfortable now that the conversation was circling back to her. With a finger, she traced a pattern on her desk. "You mean the AIDS?"

"Of course."

"It was sex, Lauren. Not needles if that was what you were thinking."

Guilt hit me yet again as I remembered my first impressions of Erin. "Your partner was infected?"

"Yeah, but I didn't know that at the time. Neither did Clyde. I was twenty-four, he was about ten years older. We went out for a month or two, then I moved on. I didn't hear from him again for many years. He called me after his diagnosis."

Oh, God, what a dreadful conversation that must have been.

"As soon as Clyde said the word *AIDS* something clicked in my head. I'd been sick off and on and had been doing my damnedest to ignore it. As it turned out, that was the worst thing I could have done. I didn't present myself to the clinic until my T-cells were already below two hundred."

"How come it happened so fast?"

"I had the virus in my system for about five years, untreated. As soon as you're infected with HIV your T4 cells begin to die. Initially the body can replace these cells and keep HIV in check. But once they drop to a certain level, the doctors usually start prescribing antiretroviral drugs. In my case, I didn't start on the drugs until I had full-blown AIDS. Since then I've been hit with one infection after another. Dr. Channing just can't keep up with them all."

Erin made it all sound so clinical. And hopeless. "Surely there are other drugs. Treatments you haven't tried…"

"Yeah, there's always something new. You should see my medicine cabinet. It's crammed with pill bottles. I can hardly keep them straight."

"But they're not working?"

Erin didn't answer at first. She twisted her arm and I saw the bruises from the blood samples that had been collected earlier that week.

"No. They're not working." She screwed up her face. "Anyway, that's not important. What matters most is that Shelley's okay. I got pregnant a few months after Clyde left. The blood work they did on me then didn't show up anything, but that's not uncommon. HIV often can't be detected for upwards of six months."

"Thank God Shelley was spared at least."

"Yeah, and I breast-fed, too, thinking I was giving her a good start, never guessing I was just increasing her odds of getting the virus."

Which hadn't happened, thank goodness. "What about the guys you slept with after Clyde? Did they get it?"

Erin shook her head. "I contacted them after my diagnosis, but lucky for them, HIV doesn't spread as easily from women as it does from men."

"Erin...can I ask a personal question?"

"I'm curious what you call a personal question after all this."

"Good point. But this is different, I think. I was just wondering if the guy who started Creative Investigations might be Shelley's father?"

"Harvey? No way. There was nothing sexual between us, Lauren. Like I've already told you, I just don't know who Shelley's father is. Those were my party days, remember."

Party days, as in no condoms, no precautions. *Oh, God, Erin. Why were you so foolish?*

"You might as well say it out loud. Yeah, I know I was stupid. The thing is, when you're young, you don't think the rules apply to you. *Wear condoms, wash your hands, don't smoke, don't drink and drive.* I broke all those rules and more."

I hadn't. I had never broken any of those rules. And I prayed my daughters wouldn't either. I needed to update the sex talk I'd had with them last year. Soon. Instinctively I checked my watch. Still an hour before I could expect them home and suddenly I was so anxious to see them. Devin might come in a little before curfew, but Jamie never did.

"Do you need to get going?"

"I should…but can I get you anything first?"

"Good God, I'm not a total invalid yet. Get out of here. I was in the middle of something, in case you hadn't noticed."

I ignored the bravado and gave my friend another hug. I noticed Erin clung to me just a little bit harder this time.

* * *

I stayed awake long enough to make sure both girls arrived home safely then crashed into bed. Though I was physically exhausted, I didn't expect to be able to sleep. Yet I did.

Saturday morning, Devin and Jamie woke before I did—something that hadn't happened in years. They squeezed into bed on either side of me.

"Can we go to Murphy's for breakfast?" Jamie asked.

"Yeah...can we?"

"I can't believe you girls like that place." I wiggled my head out from the covers. Outside the sun was shining. That seemed like a hopeful omen.

"Murphy is cool. Can we go in our pj's?" Jamie had to push the limits, like always.

"No."

"Why not?" Devin asked.

"Because it isn't proper, that's why."

"Erin doesn't worry about proper. She takes Shelley out in pajamas all the time."

All the time had to be an exaggeration, though I had noticed Erin's daughter sitting at Murphy's counter in her flannel nightgown once. "Shelley's a little girl."

"Oh, come on, Mom." Jamie grabbed my hand and

pulled. "Let's do something wild and crazy for once. You wear your jammies, too."

Devin grabbed my other hand and joined in the effort of forcibly ejecting me from my bed. We ended up all three of us on the cool wooden floor, weak with giggles.

"I'll wear a tracksuit," I compromised. I wasn't sure how they'd won this battle. But I didn't really care. Some smiles and a little laughter were worth a breach in etiquette every now and then.

Murphy noticed us the minute we walked into the diner. "Egg-white omelet and side order of fruit salad coming up," he assured the girls as he poured me my coffee.

"Nice outfit," he added, eyeing the pink designer tracksuit. "Goes great with the pearls."

"Funny." I tucked the pearls under the jacket, then doctored up my coffee. As soon as Murphy moved out of hearing range, both girls leaned in on me.

"So, Mom," Jamie said, "how was the date?"

Ah. That was why we were having this delightful mother-daughter morning.

"He seemed nice," Devin said, adding her input. "And he's a doctor. That's good, right?"

I took a sip of my coffee and considered deflecting their questions with a light-handed comment. But they were old enough for the truth.

"Actually, Burke is *Erin's* doctor."

"What? Is that how you met him?"

"Yes. And that's what I need to talk to you girls about."

I saw the apprehension in their eyes and I wished there was a way to cushion bad news, like an air bag that springs out from the dash at the moment of impact.

"Girls, I'm afraid Erin is very sick."

I could see them bracing and it broke my heart. It reminded me of that awful night when they'd come home from summer camp, tired, tanned and anxious to sleep in their own beds again. Instead, I'd made them come into the kitchen, where I'd told them that their father had left and that we'd be getting a divorce.

Jamie had affected nonchalance, a charade she hadn't been able to maintain for more than thirty seconds at which time she'd bolted for her room.

Devin had cried openly. Now she was the first one to ask a question. "What is it, Mom? Is it cancer?"

Cancer was probably the worst disease they could imagine. Until recently, it had seemed like the ultimate health hazard to me, too.

"It's not cancer, girls, though it's possible she could develop cancer as a complication. Erin has AIDS."

"No," Devin said, in a similar reaction to my earlier one.

I didn't say anything, just gave them a minute to let the news sink in.

"This really sucks," Jamie said.

"Yes, it does."

"Is she going to die, Mom?"

"I'm not sure, Devin. I hope not." It wasn't an entirely truthful answer, but it wasn't a lie, either.

Throughout breakfast I answered questions about the disease, though it turned out the girls knew more about it than I did. We discussed the effectiveness of the newest drug cocktails and I said nothing to dampen their optimism. If Erin's prognosis was as dire as I'd been led to believe, the girls would be exposed to that harsh reality soon enough.

Despite the grim subject we were discussing, the girls finished every bite of food on their plates. When they were done, Devin stood up. "I've got homework."

"Me, too. Thanks for breakfast, Mom." Jamie slipped off the stool. "Thanks, Murphy!"

From his spot behind the counter, Murphy waved at the girls as they left. He even cracked a smile, but as soon as he noticed me watching him, his face turned impassive again.

I lingered over the last of my coffee. The other night at Erin's, Murphy had seemed to be warming up to me. Today, I was persona non grata again.

I drank a little more and watched as three men dumped change from their pockets onto the counter. Once they left there was only one customer besides me.

The man with the grizzled face and dull gray hair smiled at me. I noticed a black cap beside his plate, a cane propped against his stool. So this was Stan Murdock, the old friend of Murphy's grandfather.

He slid over a couple of stools to come closer.

"You're Erin Karmeli's friend Lauren, right? I'm Stan."

He held out his hand and I shook it. "Nice to meet you, Stan."

"Likewise. That Erin's some girl, huh? Sure spiced up the neighborhood when she and her kid moved in."

"Is that right?" I wondered if Stan was referring to Erin's personality or her penchant for short skirts. Probably both.

"Oh, yeah. She's a ball of fire, that one. And she got Murph to start talking again. That was something."

The old guy held his cup, but didn't drink from it. From the way the cream had settled in a light-colored swirl on the top, I guessed the coffee was just a prop now—an excuse for Stan to prolong his time in the diner without Murphy shouting at him to order something.

"Erin got Murphy talking, did she?" I glanced over and saw Murphy behind the counter, dumping used coffee grounds into the trash. "Could have fooled me."

Stan's smile was indulgent. "You should have met him before. If he seems like a bear now, well he was a hornet then."

I shivered in mock fear. "What's Erin's secret, do you think?"

I uttered the question casually, but I was actually very interested in the answer. I was still curious about the exact relationship between those two. If anyone knew the truth, it was probably Stan.

"She reminds him of his sister."

I hadn't expected that particular answer, and it got to me. "Oh."

"Yeah. She and her kids died a long time ago—"

"Erin told me. What an awful thing." I noticed how sad Stan looked. "Did you know her, too?"

He nodded. "Sheila used to come in here with her brood every now and then. Not as often as her brother, but still, I got to know her a little. She was a crackerjack—always laughing or making a joke out of something."

Just like Erin. No wonder Murphy had been drawn to her.

"Hey, Stan, what're you doing?" Murphy was suddenly in front of us. He cleared away the breakfast dishes, talking as he worked. "No sense making friends with this one, Stan. She won't be sticking around long."

"Hey." I drew back, angry and confused at the same time. I thought we had already covered this ground. "What are you talking about, Murphy Jones?"

He didn't look at me as he rubbed an egg stain off the counter. "Come on, Lauren. Carbon Road is just a pit stop for you. My bet is that before next summer you'll be moving on."

"What if I did move out? What would you care?"

"I wouldn't. But Stan here tends to make friends for life. I was just warning him."

Murphy booted his way back to the kitchen with the dirty dishes, leaving me no time to reply.

"That man is crazy," I muttered. I tilted my head in Murphy's direction. "Did you get what that was about, Stan?"

The old man nodded. "Sure. But I'd bet I'm the only one who did."

* * *

As I was about to leave the diner, Erin breezed in the door. She'd chosen to wear a short skirt and boots today, an outfit that not that long ago had made her look ridiculously sexy.

Now she just appeared weak and thin. An impression she fostered by collapsing on a stool as if she were in dire need of oxygen.

Of course it was something else that she was here for.

"Coffee," she gasped, hamming it up for her small audience. She winked at Stan and me.

She'd no sooner said the word than Murphy had a full mug steaming by her fingers.

"You're a saint," she proclaimed, lifting the mug for a drink, not seeming to mind that the liquid was scalding.

I smiled at the performance. "I was just on my way out. Where's Shelley?"

"Lacey's watching her for a few hours so I can get a little work done."

"Oh?" I slipped back onto the stool I'd just vacated. "Is it something I can help with?"

Erin seemed annoyed. "You've got your own caseload, don't you?"

"Yes, but—"

"I'm fine. Don't worry about me."

"Okay." As I started to leave, Erin placed a hand on my arm.

"Just one more thing," she said. "I'm planning a big neighborhood dinner at my place tomorrow. Are you and the girls free?"

"How big of a dinner?" It seemed to me that Erin should be conserving her strength. Not hosting dinner parties.

"Why does it matter how big? All I asked was whether you were free. How about you, Stan?"

"Did you say dinner?" Stan rubbed his hands together gleefully. "What's on the menu?"

"Horse meat," Erin replied, sending the old guy into a deep belly laugh. She twisted to face the kitchen. "What about you, Murph?"

"I'll be there," he said quietly.

For a second his gaze met mine and again I felt the force of his disapproval. The other night I'd thought I'd finally earned his trust. Why was he still so sure that I was going to walk out on Erin?

Then the truth hit me. He'd been talking about later. *After.*

Murphy was expecting Erin to die.

CHAPTER 13

When Erin threw a dinner party, she really threw a dinner party. I spent that afternoon and the next helping her cook. We baked pies from scratch and prepared a huge chicken-enchilada casserole that looked like it would feed twenty.

And it would have to.

Besides our two families and Murphy and Stan, Erin had invited half the neighborhood.

Devin and Jamie helped Shelley decorate with balloons and streamers while Erin and I worked out last-minute details in the kitchen.

First to arrive were Iris and Nick Turchenko, bearing homemade wine and a casserole dish heaped with cabbage rolls. There were about a hundred of the fussy little delicacies and I figured Iris must have gone straight to her kitchen after Erin had delivered the invitation.

Next to come was Stella Barnes from the tattoo parlor. When Erin had stopped in to invite her, she'd been so grateful she'd offered to give Erin an Aries tattoo on her hip. But Erin, it turned out, already had a tattoo there. On Stella's heels came Denny from the hardware store, then Lacey.

The final guest to arrive—a surprise since Erin hadn't told me she'd invited him—was Dr. Burke Channing. I found out he was coming when I opened Erin's door to let him in.

Music was blaring, candles flickered and rosemary and sage incense mingled in the air along with the aroma of the food from the kitchen.

"Burke." I was shocked into silence at the sight of him on Erin's small porch.

"I hoped I was going to see you here. Erin said I probably would." He had a gift basket in his hands. Cheeses and fruit and crackers. Also a bottle of wine. "How have you been?"

He'd phoned a couple of times since our date. I hadn't returned those calls, though I'd been tempted. It felt wrong to court romance when I'd just found out

that my friend was gravely ill. It felt especially wrong
to court romance with my friend's doctor.

"I'm fine. But I hope I wasn't the reason you decided
to come tonight."

"Not the only reason." He stepped inside, clearly
not deterred by my cool welcome.

"Erin's in the kitchen." I pointed. "Back there."

I followed him through the house, thinking how
he stood out from the crowd of our other friends and
neighbors. In his trousers and suit jacket, he looked
so...so proper. I saw him hesitate when he almost
bumped into Stella.

"Hey, sorry about that," Stella said. She'd taken
a backward step without looking. Someone passed
her a napkin and she mopped the white wine from
Burke's jacket.

"No problem," Burke said. Though he didn't move
away, he still seemed to shrink from her touch. Of
course, Stella was quite a sight, with her pierced
eyebrows, nose, lips and tongue. Oddly enough, only
her ears had been spared from the piercing gun.

"Dr. Burke!" Erin shrieked. She was already on her
second or third glass of wine. "You came!" She brushed
past Stella and gave him a big hug. "Murphy, pour the
doctor a glass of wine."

I couldn't believe the scowl on Murphy's face as he silently complied. Just a minute ago he'd been behaving almost affably. My attention was diverted from the puzzle, though, at the sight of Jamie and Devin. They were on the other side of the kitchen and Mr. Turchenko was pouring wine into their glasses.

"Wait a minute," I said, but the din was too loud for old Mr. Turchenko to hear.

"Excuse me," I said to Mrs. Turchenko who was bent low in front of the oven. The rich, earthy scent of her cabbage rolls wafted out into the air. I had to wait until she had peeked under the foil, determined that nothing was burning, then closed the oven, before I could pass.

By then my girls were talking with Stella.

"A tattoo right here would be nice," Stella was saying to Jamie when I appeared by her elbow.

"Tattoo?" I repeated. "Who's thinking of getting a tattoo?"

"She's going to freak out now," Jamie told Stella. "She almost fainted the day I told her I'd gotten a second piercing in my ear. I still haven't dared show her my belly ring."

"Belly ring?"

Jamie laughed. "Chill, Mom. It was a joke. But I

do think a tattoo would look awesome right here." She pulled back the waistband of her jeans to show me a patch of skin on her hip bone. "Don't you think?"

"Oh, totally," Stella said. "You should see the one I gave my girlfriend. It would look great on you."

Girlfriend? Was Stella gay?

Oh, Lord.

I put a hand to my forehead, but Mr. Turchenko mistook the gesture as a request for more wine. He topped up my glass just in time for Lacey to trap me with my back to the refrigerator.

"Would you like a kitten?"

"I would," said Denny. He was looking at Lacey with a most affectionate expression.

"Yes, I know." She brushed him off. "But how about you, Lauren?"

"Pardon me?" The homemade wine was tasting pretty good at this point. I downed half a glassful. Erin had told me Lacey was a little loopy, but essentially good-hearted. I knew the woman had to be okay or Erin would never have let her babysit Shelley.

"I'm sure your girls would love a cute little kitten. Every family needs a pet. What do you say, Lauren?"

Stall, Lauren, stall. "Do you have a kitten?"

"Not yet, but I will have several any day now."
Lacey sighed. "I took the mother in for a friend who
had to move to Calgary—job transfer, you see. My
friend assured me that Snuggles had been spayed, but
apparently the job was done too late."

"I'm sorry about that, but I don't think we could
take on a new kitten just yet. We've had a crazy year
what with the move and all—"

"And your divorce."

"Well, yes, now that you mention it."

Lacey peered at me. "I'm sure it was devastating. But
don't worry. You're not that old and still pretty enough.
You'll find another man."

Suddenly feeling desperately thirsty, I finished the
rest of my wine, then looked over Lacey's shoulder,
hoping to catch Mr. Turchenko's gaze. Instead I caught
Murphy's. He looked amused. And totally disinter-
ested in rescuing me. As he turned away, I focused back
in on what Lacey was saying.

"...But that was me. I'm sure your experience will
be quite different. Perhaps you'll marry the doctor.
I've noticed he's been staring at you all night."

"Oh, I doubt it."

"Look for yourself." Lacey actually pointed then,
and I had no choice but to glance in that direction.

Burke, looking calm amid the chaos, was listening while Denny gestured wildly to illustrate the point of whatever story he was telling.

As our glances connected, Burke smiled. I smiled back.

"See?" Lacey poked my side. "He likes you. You should—"

But before Lacey could deliver her advice, Erin announced that dinner was served.

"Excuse me, Lacey. It's been nice talking with you."

I wasn't all that hungry, but I lined up for food anyway. There was certainly no shortage. Besides the enchilada casserole and cabbage rolls, others had contributed a smoked turkey and several salads.

"Quite an ethnic diversity," Murphy commented from behind me in the line. He passed me a paper plate, then took one for himself. "I hear you and Erin have been cooking all weekend."

"It was fun. I introduced Erin to an old relic named Eric Clapton, as well as to the ancient art of making pie pastry from scratch."

Murphy chuckled. "I forget how young she is sometimes."

It was true, I thought. When you looked into Erin's eyes, you felt as if you were seeing an old soul. Probably by Devin and Jamie's age, she had already seen and done more things than I ever had.

"Speaking of ancient arts, try one of these." Murphy handed me a warm bread roll. It smelled divine.

"You didn't make them?"

Murphy said nothing, but I recalled the homemade pizza I'd eaten at Erin's house the other day and knew that he had.

He was such a contradiction, Murphy. The way he talked, who would ever guess that he would bother to do something like bake bread or babysit for a sick friend?

When my plate was full, I found a place to sit near my daughters. "Are you guys having a good time?"

"Stanley Murdock is a riot," Jamie said. "But I'd still rather be out with my friends tonight."

"I don't mind being here," Devin said. "It's sort of like dinner at Grandma's." She glanced around the room at the motley assortment of people and food and beverages. "Only not."

I sliced a small piece of the smoked turkey. "Do you guys miss having dinner at Grandma's?"

Before we'd moved out of Rosedale, we always had Sunday dinner at my mother's, while I generally hosted my parents for all the family birthdays. When the girls were younger, they'd looked forward to these events, but as they'd entered the teen years, they'd begun balking at spending so much time with the family.

Jamie sighed. "Sort of."

Devin just shrugged.

Do you miss your father?

I didn't need to ask that question. Of course they did. But they seemed to be adjusting to their new life okay. At least I hoped they were.

"Mom," Devin whispered. "That doctor guy keeps staring at you."

I glanced across the room and noticed that Burke was sitting next to Erin. Maybe he'd been looking at me earlier, but right now he was listening to something Erin was saying. In his expression there was something so sympathetic and caring that I felt my heart soften toward him.

After everyone finished eating, the paper plates were tossed into an enormous trash can that Denny had brought from his hardware store. Stella and Iris loaded leftovers into the fridge, while Erin searched her CD collection for music.

"Come on, girls," she called to Devin and Jamie. "Help me find something to dance to."

Seconds later, Madonna was blaring through

Erin's loudspeakers, and Devin and Jamie were dancing with Shelley.

"Where are all the men tonight?" Erin asked as she sashayed through the kitchen. She looked extra skinny today, in tight jeans and a silky camisole top. Her cheeks were a vivid red, her eyes so shiny that they glowed.

"Back here, honey." Stan put down the bottle of wine he'd been using to refresh Burke's and Murphy's glasses. I took it from him to finish the job.

"Are you up to a little dancing, Stan?" Erin was already waving her arms and shimmying to the beat.

"You bet." Stan put down his glass and followed after her. "Excuse me, young fellows. Erin wants a real man tonight."

Several others joined the dancing in the other room and I was left with Murphy and Burke. Talk about an awkward triangle. The two men glared at each other and silence stretched between them as taut as the suspense in a Stephen King novel.

I felt like I ought to ask Burke to dance. But that would have left Murphy standing alone. Not that he would care, I was sure. Still, I hesitated.

The moment lingered to the point of utter painfulness. Then finally Burke set down his wineglass. "I should be going."

"Yeah, you probably should," Murphy said.

I felt like kicking him in the shin. Instead, I offered to walk Burke to his car.

"We haven't had a chance to talk all evening," Burke commented.

"It's been crazy, hasn't it?" I waited while he waved goodbye to Erin, then grabbed his jacket from the hall closet. We stepped outside and closed the door behind us. It didn't make much difference to the noise level. It was a good thing all the neighbors were at the party, or someone would definitely have called the police to complain.

"It was nice of you to come tonight," I said. "I'm sure Erin appreciated it."

"She's a great person. I only wish there was more I could do for her."

Burke pressed a button on his key chain to unlock his car door. Before I could step back, he took my hands.

I thought about taking that opening and asking more questions about Erin. But I had a feeling that Burke had nothing hopeful to say and I couldn't face hard reality tonight.

Instead I gazed into his face and thought about what a good heart he had. Good looks, too.

"Lauren?"

"Yes?"

"I couldn't take my eyes off you all night long." He pulled me closer until our faces were only inches apart. "Are you free for lunch next Saturday? I thought we could go for a walk in High Park, then grab something at one of the local delis."

It sounded like a perfectly romantic plan. "I'd love to do that."

He stared down at me and I felt the heat of attraction building. When he kissed me, it was like highschool prom with Gary all over again, that feeling of being offered something tantalizing, yet sweet and safe at the same time.

"See you tomorrow, Lauren."

As Burke drove off, I heard a door slam behind me. When I turned to rejoin the party, however, no one was in sight.

The next week, Erin was exhausted. I spent Monday in the office answering calls and dealing with administrative matters while she sprawled on the couch downstairs and complained bitterly about the boring programs on daytime television.

On Tuesday, I went with Erin to her doctor's appointment. More blood work was ordered and Erin left the appointment weaker than ever. So weak that I decided to splurge on a cab.

Wednesday morning, Erin decided she had had enough of being sick. She started work on a new case, while I kept a scheduled meeting with Sherry Frampton. Work and a series of out-of-town meetings had kept her from checking back with me since she'd asked us to get more footage of her husband.

I'd followed Martin for two of the nights she'd been in New York and had video footage as well as photographs to prove that Martin was having an affair with Sherry's boss.

We agreed to meet at a Starbucks, close to the girls' school. The coffee shop was busy and noisy, the perfect place to conduct our business.

I arrived first and purchased an Americano, thinking it would be a real treat after months of Murphy's bitter coffee. To my surprise, even this beverage tasted bland in comparison. I checked my watch. Sherry was late.

But even as I had that thought, a tall, slender woman with black hair cut in a severe bob entered the shop. Though we had never met in person, I knew from Erin's description that this was Sherry.

As the well-dressed woman scanned the crowd, I caught her eye and smiled. Sherry nodded, ordered her coffee, then joined me.

"Nice to meet you. Erin told me she'd taken on a partner."

I shook her proffered hand. Sherry had artificial nails, square-shaped and white-tipped. Once my nails had looked like that, too, but I had to say I didn't miss the twice-a-month appointments required to maintain the look.

"So did you get the film on my husband?" Sherry asked.

"Yes." I swallowed, not looking forward to this part. Sherry seemed to take for granted that her husband had been unfaithful, but the stark reality of this footage was sure to hit her hard. I felt like a heel as I handed over the tapes.

"I have some photographs as well," I added. "Would you like those, too?"

"Absolutely."

Sherry held out her hand again and I passed her the sealed manila envelope. I'd expected Sherry to take the package home, but she surprised me by inserting one of her perfect nails under the flap and slicing the envelope open. She shook out the stack of pictures.

One by one Sherry glanced through them, all without a flicker of emotion crossing her face.

"I'm sorry," I ventured. "I've just gone through a divorce myself and I know how painful this must be."

"Painful? Lauren, these photographs have made me a very happy woman. Tell Erin I'll be sending a bonus. I'll put the check in the mail tonight."

I couldn't comprehend what I was hearing, but I had to admit that Sherry looked very happy indeed. Her glossy lips were curved in a small, tight smile as she returned the photographs to the envelope. She slipped both the envelope and tapes into her briefcase.

Sherry stood, then looked down at me. I hadn't budged from my seat. This was all so strange. Not what I'd expected, at all.

Sherry sat again. "You look stunned. Let me explain."

"Okay." I waited expectantly.

"I'm in love with someone else, someone in New York. A few months ago he asked me to marry him." She tapped her briefcase lightly. "This evidence is going to ensure my divorce goes through nice and smoothly."

"Oh."

"See? Nothing to be sad about." Sherry stood for the second time. This time her smile was wide. "Thanks again, Lauren. It's been a pleasure doing business with you."

CHAPTER 14

That evening Erin and I laughed over Sherry's reaction, then watched a rerun of *House* together.

"I love that guy," Erin said during a commercial break.

The main character of the show was an arrogant, unfeeling misogynist, and the fact that Erin found him appealing certainly explained why Erin and Murphy got along so well.

"He reminds me of the new client I signed today," Erin added. "Don't worry. Not in personality—in looks."

I was worried, but not about the new client. I didn't think Erin should be working, period. Though she claimed she was feeling better, she certainly didn't look it.

A week later she had to admit that she needed to stay home in bed.

"Only for a day or two," she said, and I pretended to believe her. But less than fifteen minutes later, I heard Erin on the phone, calling her piano students to tell them they needed to find a new teacher.

Shelley started spending more time at our house, especially when one or both of the twins was at home. On Friday evening, the three girls were playing beauty salon again—still Shelley's favorite game—while I chopped carrots for homemade chicken soup. I was making a large batch since all Erin had managed to eat the past few days were liquids.

I was adding the vegetables to the stock when the doorbell rang. The girls were all upstairs, so I ran to get it, only to find Murphy on the other side of my door.

"Erin and I are going to watch *Benny & Joon*." He held up the DVD case with Johnny Depp, Mary Stuart Masterson and Aidan Quinn on the cover. "Wanna join us?"

"Sure. I've always loved that movie."

"Yeah, it's a classic."

Funny. I would have thought Murphy would be more into something like *Mission: Impossible* than a quirky drama/love story.

"What about the girls? Do you think they'd like to watch, too?"

"They're busy upstairs. Just wait while I take care of something in the kitchen and I'll be right over."

I took the pot off the stove and put it into the fridge. I could finish simmering it tomorrow morning. By the time I returned to the front door, I expected Murphy would have gone back to Erin's without me. But he was still standing in the foyer.

I slipped on a pair of shoes, then called upstairs to the girls. "If Shelley falls asleep before I get back, just give her a blanket and she can stay the night."

Shelley cheered. "Yay, another sleepover!"

Once outside I had only a moment to talk to Murphy privately. "So how's she doing?"

He shook his head, his expression grim. "I'm hoping the movie will pick her up a little. Johnny Depp seems to have that effect on women."

If that was the kind of pickup he intended, then we should be watching Johnny Depp in *Chocolat* not *Benny & Joon*. But I kept that opinion to myself as we stepped over the short hedge to Erin's porch.

Inside, Erin was on the couch in front of the television. She bent her legs to make room for me. Murphy took the armchair next to us. The lighting in the room was dim, but it couldn't mask the gaunt angles of Erin's face or her gray pallor.

My heart squeezed with pain as it always did when I was around Erin lately. This was happening too quickly. With hindsight I realized that both Burke and Murphy had tried to warn me, but I hadn't wanted to believe.

I still didn't.

"Anybody want popcorn?" Murphy asked.

Erin groaned. "Stop trying to make me eat something and just start the DVD."

The movie was as good as I had remembered but there were a few too many poignant scenes for my comfort. Perhaps it was because of the pain, in the movie and in our lives right now, that we laughed so hard at the humorous bits—Johnny Depp's character using an iron to grill cheese sandwiches for Joon; his Buster Keaton performance in the park; Benny and Joon's funny discussion about iron settings for grilled cheese.

"God, that was good," Erin pronounced when it was over.

The credits were rolling down the screen to the tune of "Five Hundred Miles" and no one was inclined to turn it off.

"Great song," Erin said. "Makes me want to dance."

I pictured her the night of the neighborhood dinner party, just two weeks previously. Erin had danced for over an hour that night. But she barely had the strength to get off the sofa now.

"I guess I should get going," Murphy said eventually. He went to get the DVD but Erin stopped him.

"Do you mind leaving it? I may watch it again later."

She wasn't sleeping well lately. Not sleeping, not eating, barely talking…

"Sure, no problem." Murphy brushed a hand over her forehead, then headed for the door. Partway there, he turned back for a moment. "Want me to bring you a coffee in the morning?"

Erin couldn't drink it. Not anymore. Still she nodded. "That would be nice."

I followed Murphy to the door. I hadn't forgotten Erin's stepfather's unexpected visit all those months ago and was always cautious to keep the doors locked.

"Good night, Murphy."

He didn't say anything, but as his eyes met mine, I saw the despair. We tried to keep our moods up for Erin's sake, but there was no pretending anymore. Not even for me.

Erin was dying.

Once Murphy was gone, I went back to the living

room. My friend's eyes were closed, her breathing was shallow and fast. I pulled up her blanket, intending to leave her to rest, but Erin's eyes flew open.

"Can we talk for a minute?"

"Of course."

I settled back on the sofa, taking Erin's legs onto my lap and gently massaging the soles of her feet.

Skin and bones and heart.

That was all that was left of her.

"I'm worried about Shelley. She's been avoiding me lately."

I didn't know what to say. Did Erin realize how much her appearance had altered in the last few weeks? The complications from her compromised immune system were multiplying now. Burke had told us at the last appointment that there was little he could do to help.

"This disease is so bloody hard," Erin said. "I love that kid so much, and she doesn't even want to hug me anymore."

"Oh, Erin." I could feel her anguish, as if it were my own.

"She won't even look at me."

"She loves you. Of course she does. But she's just a kid. And she's scared."

"I know. And I feel so bad for her. Because I can't help her with that." Erin bit her lip. "And I'm scared, too."

"Oh, Erin. We all are." The inherent injustice of her situation still tore at me. This was just so wrong. Shelley needed her mother and, frankly, I needed Erin, too. Life had just been getting good again when I'd found out about the AIDS.

Erin shimmied into a sitting position. She brushed the blanket aside and pulled her hair off her face. I watched and tried, tried so very hard, but I could not see the woman I had met on my doorstep that moving day in August.

"I have to prepare her for what's going to happen. But how in the hell am I supposed to do that? How do you tell a kid that her mother is going to die?"

The words ripped through my chest with a physical force. *Oh, Lord, how can you be so cruel?* "I don't know, Erin. There must be counselors at the hospital who could help?"

"Strangers." Erin shook her head. "I'm not taking Shelley to talk to strangers. She's already mixed-up enough. The poor kid…she doesn't even know what death is."

"Do any of us?" My intellectual family had never

fostered any religious beliefs in me. Gary's flight to India hadn't exactly bolstered my faith in the spiritual world, either.

"I used to think it was just the end, period," Erin said. "Now I'm not so sure."

Once I had thought the same thing. I hadn't believed in a spirit that would go on after the physical body had died.

But looking into Erin's fevered face right now, a face streaked with tears and lined with pain, those beliefs no longer worked for me. How could I tell my friend that this was it—there would be nothing more?

I couldn't believe it myself.

All this love and energy that was Erin couldn't just disappear from the earth without a trace.

I took Erin's hands and held them. I wished I was stronger. That I could somehow funnel strength from myself into my friend's weak body. "If anything can survive death, it would have to be a mother's love."

"Yes," Erin whispered. "That's the way I feel, too. Shelley brought me everything good that I ever had. All I wanted, from the moment she was born, was to give her those good things back. I never wanted her to feel alone and scared the way I did when I was little."

"You're a great mom, Erin. Anyone who saw you and Shelley together would know it."

"Coming from you, that means a lot. I wish you could feel how my heart explodes when I think of her."

"I know. I *do* feel it." I felt it for Erin and Shelley. And I felt it for my own kids, too. Even though the twins were older now, I ached for every disappointment that came their way.

When Gary had told me he was leaving, my first thought hadn't been for myself, but for Jamie and Devin.

My babies, I'd thought. *They're losing their family. The foundation of their safe little world is about to crumble.*

And there was nothing I'd been able to do about it.

At least Devin and Jamie's father was still alive. One day he *would* return from India. They *would* see him again. And in the meantime, they at least had postcards.

What would Shelley have? *Who* would Shelley have?

Erin must have been thinking the same thing. "Besides me, Shelley doesn't have any family."

I thought of Erin's mother and stepfather. Definitely not an option. Was there anyone else?

"I did some research on this a while ago. In the absence of family to take her in, Shelley's going to become a ward of the state."

That would mean a foster home. I shook my head, knowing that wouldn't be right for Shelley.

"Ever since I found out I was sick, I've been worrying about this."

Erin's gaze was locked with mine and in that moment I understood what my friend was saying to me. Erin had known this moment was coming months ago. That was why Erin had befriended me. And offered me a stake in the business.

Because of Shelley.

It was all about Shelley and always had been.

"You're a good person, Lauren. Way better than I could ever be."

"That isn't true. You're too hard on yourself."

"Maybe. But the first time I saw you with your girls I knew that I had found Shelley's salvation. I know it's a lot to ask. We haven't known one another long. But you're pretty much the nicest person I've ever met."

My tears were overflowing now. I held on to Erin's hands tighter.

"Shelley feels safe with you. She adores your

daughters. She's a good kid, Lauren. She won't be much trouble."

I started to sob.

"Murphy said he'd take her, but Shelley needs a mother. I'm sorry I don't have much money saved up. No trust fund, you know?"

I couldn't handle this anymore. "Shut up about the trust fund, Erin. I'll take her. I'd love to take her."

In the back of my mind a voice told me I was crazy. I could barely look after myself and my own daughters. And Shelley was so much younger than the twins. It would be more than a decade before she'd be ready to even consider moving out of the house.

But the words were out, and what was more, I knew I couldn't have lived with myself if I'd reacted in any other way.

The next morning I had a talk with the girls. First I called the twins into my bedroom and told them what Erin had asked of me. Of us. I warned them that having a six-year-old to take care of was going to be more work for all of us. And there would be times when she seemed more annoying than cute.

"This is a big decision," I said. "Are you girls okay with it?"

"Shelley doesn't have anyone else," Devin said. "We have to do this, Mom."

"It'll be okay," Jamie agreed. "We can handle it."

I made sure they understood that money would now be spread thinner. And that, at least for a while, there'd be a need to share bedrooms.

Neither one complained. I was so proud of them.

Next I spoke with Shelley. The little girl was dressed for school, sitting at the kitchen table eating her cereal. She looked so tiny and innocent. My stomach twisted as I sat in the chair next to her.

"Shelley, I've had a talk with your mom and we've agreed that anytime she's too sick to take care of you, you're going to stay here with us."

"And when she's better, I go home."

I swallowed. "Yes."

That night I had plans to go out to dinner with Burke. I felt guilty about how much I was looking forward to the break. Yes, I needed to relax and have a little fun.

But what about Erin? There would be no break for her.

She wouldn't hear of me canceling though. "Don't worry about me. Murphy's coming over. And Jamie already said Shelley could hang out with her tonight."

I was so impressed with the way my daughters had handled everything. When I'd told them about the situation, I'd prepared them for the possibility that Erin had only weeks now, probably less than that. I was now taking Shelley to and from school, packing her lunch, washing her clothes. But it was the girls' company Shelley seemed to crave most.

I slipped on a black dress I hadn't worn since I'd moved to Carbon Road. It seemed a little loose, and I realized a lot of my clothes had felt that way lately. Maybe a nice meal out wasn't such an indulgence, after all. I didn't want to add to the problems around here by wearing myself out and getting sick, too.

Burke picked me up at seven. It was the first time I'd seen him in a suit and he looked utterly elegant. As he looped his arm for me to hold onto, I noticed our reflection in the foyer mirror.

We make a nice-looking couple.

Our dinner was delicious, the conversation easy. By mutual accord we steered clear of discussing Erin or anything related to her disease and prognosis. All evening long, Burke kept sending me signals that he was ready for our relationship to progress to the next level. I may not have dated in over twenty years, but there was no mistaking the signs.

I didn't agonize over my decision. I'd been seeing Burke for six weeks now. It was time to find out if the chemistry between us was leading anywhere.

He took me to his house, which was very neat and organized. I wasn't surprised to see a book on feng shui on the coffee table. He offered me a drink, but I refused.

I was excited, but also nervous, definitely unsure how to proceed. Would we neck in the living room first, then move on to the bedroom? At what point would the clothes come off? Was I wrong to assume he would have the condom situation covered, so to speak?

Burke finessed my anxieties by putting on a CD and pulling me close for a dance. His choice of music—a jazz standard by Diana Krall—wasn't exactly inspired, but I did like being in his arms.

I'd forgotten how wonderful it was to be held by a man. His arms curved securely around my back, while mine went around his shoulders. Burke was just tall enough that I could rest my face on his shoulder. I loved the detergent-and-starch scent of his shirt. It reminded me of Gary....

But I wasn't supposed to be thinking of Gary right now, was I? Yet as the night progressed, as Burke led me to his room, kissed me, then lowered me gently to his bed, thoughts of Gary kept coming.

Gary didn't kiss like this.

Gary never used to touch me there.

Gary didn't usually talk this much.

Burke was a communicative lover, which was probably a great thing if a woman was used to it. "Tell me what you like?" he kept asking. "How does this feel?"

In the end, it didn't really matter. The whole thing was over too fast and I was pretty sure I wasn't the only one who hadn't enjoyed it all that much.

"I'm sorry," Burke said, trailing his finger down my bare arm. "I think there were four people in the bed that time."

I laughed with relief at his honesty. I couldn't have stood it if he'd tried to pretend that everything had been just wonderful.

The second time was better. In fact, it came pretty close to wonderful. I rested my head on his chest and tried not to think about Erin.

Erin, who would never make love to a man again.

Or bake another apple pie.

Or see her daughter graduate from grade school, let alone high school and university.

Burke shifted so he could see my face. "Thinking about Erin?"

I nodded.

"I'm so sorry. As a doctor I hate feeling powerless. But there's nothing more I can offer."

"There must be something we can do for her."

"There is, but you may not want to hear it."

I waited.

"Help her prepare for death."

I closed my eyes. "You're right. I didn't want to hear that." When Burke said nothing, I relented. "Okay, I can't keep my head in the sand. I want to help her, even if it's hard. But how can I help Erin deal with death?"

"There are practical matters that shouldn't be ignored. You can make sure her legal affairs are in order. And you can also ask her if there's anyone from her family she'd like to say goodbye to. It's very common for my AIDS patients to have unresolved issues with their families. Ultimately their passing is much more restful if they are able to talk to the people they love before they go."

"As far as I know, the only family Erin has is her slimy stepfather and her mother."

"Does her mother know she has AIDS?"

"I asked Erin that the other day. She said no. When I asked if she wanted me to tell her she just laughed."

I propped myself up on my elbows. "She said her mother wouldn't care."

"She might be right."

"Yes."

"Or—"

Burke didn't say anything more, but I knew what he was thinking and I agreed. Erin's mother ought to be given a chance.

CHAPTER 15

On Sunday Erin had a good day. She played with Shelley all morning. After lunch, she wanted to go upstairs to her office.

"I need to sort through a few things."

Murphy and I looked at each other. We were spending most of our free time at Erin's house now, as were the twins. Erin liked having lots of people around.

"I'd like to go with her," I said quietly.

Murphy nodded. "I'll take Shell to the park. She hasn't been outside all day."

So many things about Erin broke my heart these days. Watching her struggle up the stairs was another of them. Erin moved like a fragile, old lady now. Though she rarely complained, it was obvious that she was in constant pain.

In her office, though, I saw a flash of her former energy as she booted up the computer, then unlocked the bottom drawer of her desk.

"I've been trying to keep up with everything," I said, thinking that Erin was worried about the business. "I sent in the last batch of background checks on Friday and I'm going to pay some of our outstanding accounts tonight."

"That's good." Erin sounded distracted. She pulled several file folders from the drawer. She laid them on her desk, then turned back to the computer and opened a Word document.

It was her will.

My first instinct was to withdraw, but when I headed for the door, Erin frowned.

"We need to talk about a few things, Lauren. Can you shut the door?"

My body reacted with a definite "fight-or-flight" response. My palms began to sweat, my heart raced. I didn't want to talk to Erin about these sorts of things, but neither had I forgotten what Burke had told me on the weekend.

Preparing for death was something Erin could no longer avoid. As her friend, the least I could do was help.

"I'm going to make the changes to my will to reflect

the conversation we had about Shelley the other night. Unless you've changed your mind?"

There was no judgment in Erin's expression as she asked that question and I realized this was my last possible out. I hadn't mentioned anything about assuming guardianship for Shelley to Burke. Now I wondered what he would have said if I'd asked his opinion.

Perhaps I should phone him now?

As soon as I had the thought, I rebelled against it. This was my decision. Mine and the twins'. I'd already talked to them and they'd agreed that this was something our family had to do.

"I haven't changed my mind."

Erin sighed, obviously relieved. "I'm leaving you all my financial assets, my business and title to this house. In the long run it probably won't be enough, but at least it will help."

"Don't worry, Erin. We're going to be fine. I'll make sure Shelley has everything she needs, everything that Devin and Jamie get, she will get, too."

Erin swallowed and nodded. "Thank you," she said softly. Then she began to scroll through the document on her computer screen, adding my name wherever the guardian was mentioned.

When Erin was finished she hit Print and soon the will was spilling, page by page, onto the desk.

"I need to tell you something else." Erin turned from the computer and faced me calmly. "I've given Murphy my power of attorney for personal care. So, if I should go into a coma or my pain relievers affect my alertness, or whatever, he'll be the one to make my decisions. He knows what I want."

I pulled in a long deep breath. I wanted to thank her for picking Murphy for that job. I didn't think I was strong enough to handle it myself.

But even as I had that thought, I realized it was cowardly. "Erin—what *do* you want?"

"For this to end. I'm ready, Lauren, you know I am. I've told Burke, and I've told Murphy, too, that I don't want any further treatment or life-saving measures."

"Erin." My voice broke over her name. "You've got to keep hoping. You can't give up."

She smiled sadly. "It isn't fun anymore. Nothing is. And I don't want to draw this out any longer than necessary. This isn't how I want Shelley to remember me."

It wasn't right. I wanted Erin to fight for as long as possible. I wasn't ready for her to give up. I just wasn't. I could feel my tears welling and falling down my cheeks.

"I'm not ready to lose you."

Erin's face crumbled for a second, then she pulled herself together. "Thank you."

I sucked in a big breath. If Erin could be this brave, so could I. I gathered the pages of the will, then stapled them. "What about your mother? Do you plan on leaving her anything?"

Erin nodded. "I've made a small provision for her. She'll only drink it away, but what can I do?"

"Are you still certain you don't want to see her?"

"Oh, yeah. Trust me, that would be an ugly scene."

"You don't think she would come if she knew you were sick?"

"Dying," Erin corrected. "Not *sick*. And sure my mother would come. She'd try to talk me into leaving everything to her...including Shelley. God knows what damage she and my stepfather would inflict on *her*."

I winced at the horrible thought.

Erin tucked the document into the file with her power of attorney for personal care. "We'll need to find witnesses and get this signed later today."

I hated the urgency in her voice. Hated the fact that Erin seemed to sense that her time was fading fast.

And yet, I knew that, once again, Erin was right.

* * *

After sorting through her legal and financial affairs, Erin was exhausted. She settled back on the couch and soon fell asleep. I covered her with a blanket, pausing to check her forehead. She was running a fever constantly now.

Murphy was still out with Shelley. The twins wouldn't be home from school for at least two hours. There was lots of work waiting to be done, but I felt one task in particular had to take priority now.

I opened the file that contained Erin's documents and looked for the mention of her mother. As I'd hoped, Erin had included an address. I jotted it down on a piece of scrap paper, wrote a note for Murphy explaining that I would be back by four, then set out for the bus.

As I walked, I justified to myself what I was about to do. Erin didn't want to contact her mother because she was certain that her mother wouldn't care. But what if she was wrong? What if her mother leaped at the chance to make final amends with her daughter?

I knew I couldn't live with myself unless I made an effort to find out if that was possible.

The address was for an area of the city north of Sheppard and west of Bathurst. It was not the nicest, nor the safest part of Toronto by any means, and I was glad I had chosen to carry out this errand in the daytime.

It took forty-five minutes for me to finally find the shabby apartment building where Erin's mother and stepfather lived. Hopelessness and despair seemed to peer from every window at me as I passed.

The line of buzzers on a panel by the door had no numbers or names to identify the tenants. It didn't matter anyway. The front lock was broken. All I needed to do was walk inside and search for unit number five.

Out on the street I hadn't felt too vulnerable. In here though, I felt trapped and exposed, all at the same time. I kept remembering the one time I'd met Erin's stepfather and I prayed that I would find Mrs. Karmeli alone.

I had to knock several times before the door finally opened, spewing an odor of stale alcohol into the hall. A woman in a fuzzy housecoat peered out at me. She looked cranky, as if she'd just woken up.

"Who the hell are you?"

There was to be no polite preamble. I'd have to dive straight in. "I'm a friend of your daughter's."

"Is that a fact?" Mrs. Karmeli's over-plucked

eyebrows rose even higher on her forehead. Once she'd probably been attractive like her daughter. But the years—and the alcohol—had been hard on her.

"I just—I'm her neighbor, Lauren Holloway, and I thought you should know that Erin isn't well."

The older woman's sharp features collapsed in a frown. "She got cancer?"

When I didn't say anything, Mrs. Karmeli took my silence for assent. "I always told her she was an idiot for smoking. Still, I thought she quit after she had the brat."

Involuntarily I took a step back.

"If she thinks I'm going to come and help take care of her, she's got her nerve. That girl tried to steal my husband out from under my nose. Tell her I haven't forgot that. I never will."

The next backward step I took was not involuntary. Nor was the next or the next. Without another word to Erin's poor excuse for a mother, I turned and raced to the entrance and the relative freshness of the inner-city air.

That evening a parade of visitors came through Erin's house, as if by secret agreement. First was Stan Murdock who sat in a chair next to Erin and held her hand while he told her stories about Murphy as a young man.

Next was Stella from the tattoo parlor. She told Erin about one of the customers she'd had that day, a poor, frightened teenager who'd come wanting a tongue piercing to defy his father, but who'd ended up fainting in the waiting room instead.

Burke dropped in for half an hour. He spoke quietly with Erin, took her temperature and listened to her lungs and her heart, then talked some more. When he was done, he came into the kitchen where I was making a second pot of coffee for all the visitors.

I set down the bag of grounds and went to him. He placed his arms gently on my shoulders.

"She looks really bad, doesn't she?"

His mouth tightened compassionately, then he said, "I'm sorry."

I dropped my head to his chest and just stood there, drawing deep breath after deep breath while Burke stroked my back.

When I finally could face him again without crying, he kissed my cheek. "I'll see you tomorrow. Make sure you get some rest. This is hard on you, too, you know."

Next came Iris and Nick Turchenko, along with Denny Stavinsky. The Turchenkos brought a basket of fresh fruit from their market, and I set it on the table, wondering if Erin would be able to enjoy any of the beautiful produce. I couldn't remember the last time Erin had eaten anything other than warm water and my homemade chicken soup.

"Thanks for coming," Erin told the older couple.

"Is there anything we can do, dear?" Iris took her hand and bent low to wait for an answer.

"Actually, yes. I need two witnesses for my will. Lauren—"

Having anticipated the request, I laid the document by Erin and passed her a pen. When she was done, Iris and Nick added their signatures as well.

"All done." Erin sank back to the cushions with a sigh.

The visitors stayed long enough to drink one cup of coffee apiece and then they left. Since Shelley was sleeping over with Devin and Jamie again, and Murphy had decided to spend a few hours at his neglected diner, Erin and I were now alone.

"Tired?" I asked, as I tried to arrange the pillows so Erin would be comfortable.

"You have no idea." She closed her eyes and I thought she had drifted off until she spoke again. "Lacey came by this morning. She mentioned her cat had kittens a few weeks ago."

"Oh, good. That's all she needs is more cats."

Erin's chest heaved with her effort to laugh. "I think she plans to give most of them away. Lauren—?"

"Yes?"

"You wouldn't consider taking one, would you? For Shelley?"

The weight that seemed to press on my heart all the time now suddenly became heavier.

"I think it would be a good distraction…" Erin's voice started as a whisper, then faded to nothing. Her translucent eyelids fluttered, then she closed them again. A moment later she had dipped back into sleep.

For a long while I stood there and watched her. Even in sleep, Erin's body twitched with pain. Her chest rattled with each shallow breath. According to Burke, her body's immune system was completely compromised. She had no defenses left.

It was just a question of time.

CHAPTER 16

The next day Burke dropped in on Erin at the end of his office hours. I was in the kitchen preparing another batch of chicken soup, pretending to myself that Erin would be around long enough to eat it. I heard the murmur of voices—mostly Burke's—for about fifteen minutes. Then he popped into the kitchen and gave me a kiss.

"Lauren, honey, I'm sorry but it's time for her to go to the hospital. She isn't getting enough oxygen."

I had known I would hear bad news. I just hadn't known what form it would take.

"Erin doesn't want to go, Burke. She doesn't want to be separated from Shelley."

"Yes, she told me that."

I stopped stirring and searched his eyes. "I bet she did."

"She's still Erin, thank goodness, but I'm not sure for how much longer. One of the complications that I'm afraid she's developed is an infection of the brain that we call PML—progressive multifocal leukoencephalopathy. So far she's lost some vision and is experiencing problems with motor control. Mental deterioration won't be far behind."

"Oh, Burke." Wasn't there any good news? "Is the pneumonia getting any better?"

"No. It won't, Lauren. The best thing at this point is to get her into the hospital and do what we can to ease her suffering."

He came up behind me and squeezed my shoulders. "I wish I could offer you some hope. For Erin's sake and for yours."

"I know, Burke." This was hard on him, too. Hard on us all. I set the wooden spoon on the stove and turned to give him a hug. As his arms enveloped me, I had the illusion of safety and comfort.

But as soon as he pulled away, harsh reality returned.

"I have a meeting tonight," Burke said.

I knew he sat on several charitable boards but I didn't ask which one he was attending tonight.

"Will you talk to her? Convince her that it's the right thing to do?"

"I'll try. I don't know if she'll listen." I'd have to talk to Murphy, too. He'd called earlier to say he'd drop over around eight. His opinion was important since he was the one who would be in charge if Erin did start to lose her ability to function mentally.

It was a prospect that made me want to collapse to the floor and weep.

That evening, after Shelley had fallen asleep, Murphy and I decided to talk to Erin. We pulled up chairs and sat as close to her as possible. Erin reached out for our hands. Her grip was surprisingly strong.

Or was it desperate?

"I'm not going to the hospital."

I glanced at Murphy before saying, gently, "I'm not sure we have a choice at this point."

Erin closed her eyes and refused to say anything else.

After about ten minutes, I gave up. "I need to go home and spend some time with my daughters." The last few nights I'd slept in Shelley's room, while Devin and Jamie had taken care of Shelley at our house. It was an arrangement that couldn't continue for long.

Devin and Jamie were only fifteen. They couldn't keep shouldering the responsibility of caring for a six-year-old, while watching a family friend slipping down the slope toward death.

"I can stay tonight if you like," Murphy offered.

"That would be great. Thank you."

"Hey." He put a hand on my shoulder. "We're in this together."

I stared back at him. That was the nicest thing he had ever said to me.

He must have seen the surprise in my expression. "I was wrong about you, Lauren. I thought when you found out what was wrong with Erin, you'd bolt. But you didn't. You've done the exact opposite of bolting."

"Do you know she's asked me to take Shelley?"

He gave me an assessing look. "The day you moved into the neighborhood she had you pegged for that."

"Yeah. I finally figured that out." I didn't know if I should feel angry or used. Maybe I had reason to. But I couldn't blame Erin. Put in her shoes, I'd be just as desperate to find a good home for my daughters.

"I told her she was making a mistake. That she shouldn't pin her hopes on you."

"You really didn't think much of me, did you?"

"Like I said, I was wrong."

His hand was still on my shoulder, but it was no

longer a reassuring, bracing grip. His fingers had relaxed and for one crazy second I imagined him sliding that hand down my back, then pulling me closer....

I closed my eyes. *Get a hold of yourself, Lauren. What the heck are you thinking?*

The sound of the doorbell startled us both.

I glanced at the time on the stove. Who would be visiting at this hour? With fearful thoughts of Erin's stepfather, I followed Murphy to the door.

But it was only kindly old Stan Murdock.

"What's up, Stan?" Murphy stepped back to make room for the other man to come inside.

"Erin called. Said she needed to see me."

He had his hand in his pocket, but when he noticed me looking, he pulled it out. A small bulge remained in the pocket and I wondered what he had in there.

"Want me to take your jacket?" Murphy asked.

Stan shook his head on his way through to the living room. "How's my girl?" He took the chair that Murphy had been sitting in earlier and reached for Erin's hand.

"Stan." That was all Erin said, but I could hear the relief in her voice.

"I'm here, baby. Don't worry. I'll take care of things

now." Stan turned to them. "Why don't you guys go home for a spell? You both look like you could use a good night's sleep. I'll stay with her tonight."

"Lauren's got to go home to the kids," Murphy said. "But why don't I stay, too? We can make it a party."

"No." Erin shifted herself into a prone position. "Go home, Murph. You, too, Lauren."

"What? You sick of us already?"

"You bet I am." Her head collapsed into the pillow.

"Seriously, I can stay with her tonight," Stan said.

Murphy shrugged. "Okay, but I'm warning you, she snores."

A flicker of a smile crossed Erin's lips. She held out her hand and Murphy took it in his.

"I love you, Murph."

"Ditto."

"Ditto? I'm dying and *ditto* is the best you can come up with?"

"Pretty much."

Erin laughed. "Well, get out of here you two. I love you both but Stan and I have stuff to do."

I went to give her a kiss. Erin whispered something so quietly I couldn't hear it. "What did you say?" I asked softly.

"You're the best friend I ever had, Lauren. The very best."

"You, too, Erin. You are, too."

I opened my eyes at 9:37 the next morning. I stared at the digital display on my alarm clock for several seconds, unable to believe it could be so late.

"Why didn't you go off?" I asked the clock. Like it could answer.

I leaned forward to check if I had set it properly. That's when I saw the note on my night table.

Mom, we thought you could use some sleep so we turned off your alarm. I'm making all our lunches and Jamie is walking Shelley to school. See ya later!

What sweethearts.

I dragged myself out of bed and headed for the shower. My head was fuzzy, my stomach queasy. I'd never had a really bad hangover before, but I imagined this was what it would feel like.

Once I was dressed, I headed downstairs, not sure what to do. I could make myself something to eat, or go to the diner. But the thought of food made me sick.

I need to check on Erin.

I'd half expected a call from Stan last night, or at

least early this morning. But maybe Murphy had spelled him for me.

I opened the front door and stepped outside. The day looked bleak. Gray skies, bare trees, dead grass. November had to be one of the ugliest months of the year.

I stepped over the hedge, then hesitated before trying Erin's door.

For some reason I wasn't ready to go inside. *I can't face her. Not yet.*

I sat on the porch steps and wrapped my arms around my legs. The cold wind chased up the sleeves of my sweater and down my neck to my chest. I welcomed the freezing sensation. Wished I could get so cold that I'd lose all the feeling in my heart for a while. Just long enough to find the strength to be cheerful for Erin.

As I sat there I noticed a tall man with long, lean legs and broad shoulders coming down the street. He had on jeans and a black jacket with a gray scarf looped around his neck.

It was Murphy.

I waited for him to walk up to me. When he held out his hands, I let him pull me up. I could hardly look him in the eyes, knowing I'd see the same heavy-hearted sadness that I was feeling.

"I guess we'd better see what kind of night she had."
I let go of his hands and started for Erin's door for the
second time.

"Wait."

I turned back to Murphy. "Why?"

"Didn't you see the ambulance?"

For a shocked moment my brain wouldn't work.
Then, all too soon, electrons were firing again. "Did
Stan call 911? What hospital did they take her to?"

Erin was going to be so angry. She'd been adamant
about her decision to die at home.

Oh, no.

Murphy was still standing on the sidewalk. His arms
hung loosely at his side. He looked lost. Afraid. Sorry.

Oh, no.

I took the steps slowly. When I reached the ground,
Murphy held out his hands again. This time I let him
crush me to his chest.

"When did it happen?"

"Five o'clock this morning. She just fell asleep, Stan
said. It was very peaceful."

I thought about the little something that Stan had
been carrying in his jacket and was thankful.

CHAPTER 17

When someone says time passed in a fog, what they really mean is that they have so much stuff going on inside their brain that their sensory perceptions get lost in the mayhem. I remembered a few things about the days that followed, but not much.

Telling Shelley her mom was gone was the hardest. "But I want her! I want my mommy!"

"Oh, baby." I held her and soothed her and sang songs I thought I'd forgotten over a decade ago.

Despite having spent so much time with Devin and Jamie, suddenly Shelley clung to me. I kept her with me all the time. At night Shelley slept in my bed and in the morning, every morning, we went to Murphy's for breakfast.

The twins came, too, even though it meant rolling

out of bed at least fifteen minutes earlier than usual. The four of us would line up at the counter and Murphy would give each of the girls their own custom breakfast, while I would receive the standard two-egg special.

And coffee.

I couldn't remember ever drinking so much coffee in my life. I craved it all the time and suspected that the caffeine was all I was running on.

Thank God Murphy was there to handle the details of the cremation and the organizing of the memorial service and a hundred other administrative tasks.

"Just take care of Shelley and your girls," he'd say to me whenever I offered to help.

On the day of the memorial service, Devin and Jamie didn't go to school. Putting on a black skirt and jacket in my room, I wondered if I'd ever been through a more awful time.

Even the divorce from Gary hadn't been this hard.

I was scared to imagine what my life was going to be like without Erin. We'd only known each other a short while, but she had brought so much to me in that time. Fun, excitement, happiness. And true friendship.

She'd shown me what I had once not understood

was possible…. A woman could create a family for her children all on her own.

Erin had done that, and more. She'd filled a space in her community, been someone who mattered to people who didn't have a lot of warmth in their lives.

It was hard to step inside Erin's house and feel how empty it was without her. No curry simmering on the stove. No Black Eyed Peas on the sound system. No funny, caustic Erin running around doing three jobs at once.

The service was intimate and irreverent, just what Erin would have liked. Burke sat with the girls and Murphy and me in the front row. Our neighbors spread out in the seats behind us. Among them were several of the contacts that Erin had introduced me to: Jerry from the local police station, Catherine from the *Toronto Star*, Alex from city hall.

I could picture each of their business cards from Erin's Rolodex. But I could barely speak to any of them.

When the service was over, everyone went to Murphy's for coffee and sandwiches. Upstairs, in his apartment, more sustaining liquor choices were available. That was where I headed as soon as I could.

I settled myself in one of Murphy's comfortable

leather chairs and didn't move. For a while Shelley sat in my lap, until Devin convinced her to go with her and Jamie to the park.

"We'll feed her dinner and put her to bed, Mom," Devin whispered.

"If she cries for me—"

"We'll come and get you. Promise."

"Thanks, honey." I sank back into the chair as Burke came into the room. He had a plate of sandwiches and a cup of coffee from downstairs. He put them in front of me.

"Try to eat something."

"I will." I felt badly for him, guessing that the service had probably been a painful reminder of his wife. When he sat in the sofa next to me, I reached over and squeezed his hand.

But that was all I could offer in the way of sympathy. Oddly I felt both empty and heavy at the same time.

Slowly the guests left. Burke was one of the last.

"Let me drive you home."

I didn't want him to do that. I wasn't sure why. "I think the walk will be good for me."

"I want to make sure you get there safely."

"It's only a block. I'll call later tonight."

Finally he relented. After planting a kiss on my

cheek he headed for the stairs, passing Murphy who was on his way up.

"Thanks for everything, doc."

"I'm glad I had the chance to know Erin. No, don't bother turning around. I'll see myself out."

I had barely seen Murphy all day. He'd been acting as host, filling coffee mugs and handing out food. Now he sank into the seat Burke had just vacated and leaned his head back.

"Thank God that's over."

Poor Murphy had to be both mentally and physically exhausted, like me. But unlike Murphy, I wasn't glad the memorial service was over. Because that meant it was time to start regular life again.

But I didn't have a regular life anymore. This was just like when Gary had left—my life was full of holes. No more dinners with Erin, drinks on the porch, shared coffees at Murphy's.

I glanced at Murphy, startled by a realization. "You're wearing a suit." This was the first time I'd seen him in anything but a plaid shirt and jeans.

He looked down at himself as if he couldn't remember what he'd put on that morning. "A change is good now and then, huh?"

"No, it isn't. Sorry—I don't mean that there's

anything wrong with your suit. You look good in it, actually. It's just that I don't like change. I'm sick of change."

"Is that why you always wear those pearls?"

I touched the strand like it was my talisman. "Gary gave me these for our tenth wedding anniversary. The girls were seven then, just a year older than Shelley. It was a very happy period in my life. Pretty much the happiest."

"You'll have happy times again."

A month ago I'd believed that, too. But now… "It doesn't feel like it."

"I know."

I turned my head so I could see him more clearly. The poor man looked…like hell. And then I remembered his sister and her children and all the losses that this day must have reminded him of.

"I'm sorry, Murphy. I've been so selfish. I never even thought about the terrible memories you have to deal with."

He looked at me quizzically. "Someone told you about my sister?"

"Erin did. And Stan."

"Well, that was a long time ago. Her kids would have graduated by now."

For the first time I noticed a picture frame on a corner table. I got up to look at it. The picture swiveled so you could see both sides. On one side was a photograph of a woman with two toddlers. I could see Murphy's coloring and his firm jawline in the woman.

I flipped the frame over and Erin smiled up at me. She had Shelley sitting on her shoulders. Both were laughing.

Pain sliced through my chest. I hadn't cried all day, I'd been too numb, but now my tears flowed so fast I was blinded. I put out a hand, hoping to get my bearings.

And there was Murphy.

"Lauren."

There was something in the way he said my name. I stepped in his direction, and he must have done the same thing at the same time, because suddenly we were holding each other and he was pressing his face to the top of my head.

"No," I said. "No, no, no!" With each *no*, I held him tighter and he seemed to understand that I wasn't objecting to being held, but to the fates that had taken our friend from us.

The part of me that had been numb and empty just moments ago was filled with rage and I wanted to take that picture and throw it against the wall.

Instead I lifted my face to Murphy's, and as if the whole thing had been choreographed, he bent to me at the same time. And we kissed.

It was a hard kiss, a demanding kiss.

It said, *Forget all this, everything that's happened. Only feel what's happening now, in this moment.*

My body was suddenly on fire with a level of desire I could hardly relate to. If Murphy stopped kissing me, I knew I would die, just like Erin. I pressed my body into his and instant heat flared into urgent need.

Murphy's hands slid up my skirt. I tugged at his trousers. *Is this me? Can this possibly be me?*

I wouldn't let myself think any further than that. The thing was to *feel* not to *think*.

Murphy's body was beautiful…strong, broad, utterly male. I felt engulfed by him, and yet powerful. I could feel his wild response to me and that made me wild, too.

Suddenly I was calling, "Yes, yes, yes." Every cell in my body craved him as he carried me back to the sofa. I touched him while he ripped open a condom.

The rubber almost spoiled everything. I felt an instant association to AIDS, to Erin, to death and disease.

But then Murphy kissed me again, and I was able to push all that to the background. He lifted my legs, one to each shoulder, and trailed his tongue down my thigh.

Maybe he'd thought I wasn't ready. But when he saw how wet I was, he groaned. A moment later he was cradling my head and pushing himself inside.

We rocked against each other, grinding and thrusting like wild animals. I could feel the ascent building and I tried to stop it.

It was too soon. I didn't want this to end.

But the tipping point had been reached. As pleasure exploded inside me, I felt Murphy grip my hair and give out a low, guttural moan.

There.

Just like that it was over. Murphy, hot and sweaty, rolled off me. I stared at his ceiling, his plain white ceiling, and wondered what had happened to all the stars I'd been seeing just a minute ago.

"Don't feel bad about this," Murphy said.

"I don't." Not yet, anyway. "I've read about people responding this way after a funeral. Sex makes them feel alive. Helps take away some of the fear."

Murphy zipped up his pants, then smoothed down my skirt. "It worked for me."

I let him pull me up. "Me, too."

"Good. It's important not to feel guilty. Erin would have understood."

Undoubtedly. But would Burke?

Murphy led me to the bathroom. With a warm, damp washcloth, he cleaned me up, touching my most intimate body parts with the gentle detachment of a nursing-home assistant.

He was so matter-of-fact about all this. I did my best to follow his lead. As soon as I was together again, composed—at least outwardly—he led me down the stairs.

At the door to the street I tried to let go of his arm. "I'll be fine—"

"I know," he said. But still he walked me right to the door of my home. It was dark now and I tried not to notice the unlit windows on Erin's side of the house.

I turned to Murphy and wondered if he would try to kiss me good-night.

But I should have known better. As soon as my door was unlocked, Murphy pulled away. "See ya," he called casually, before loping down the stairs and moving briskly in the direction of the diner.

So that's how it would be.

I knew I ought to feel grateful.

* * *

The first thing I did was check on Shelley. The little girl was fast asleep in my bed. The twins were doing homework in their rooms. Each returned my hug, but declined my offer to make them hot chocolate.

I had tidied the kitchen and was just about to go upstairs for a bath, when the doorbell rang. As usual, I checked the peephole. It was Lacey. She was carrying a basket and a big shopping bag.

"Hi, sweetie," she said when I opened the door. "I know you're tired but I had to give you this. It's important."

"Come in."

Lacey stepped inside, then uncovered the basket. A ball of fur—a kitten—let out a little meow.

"Oh, Lacey. She's so cute. But—"

Lacey passed me the basket. I had no choice but to hold it. The kitten made another little noise and I couldn't resist scooping it out and cupping it in my hands.

"She's so soft."

"Isn't she?" Lacey sorted through the contents of her shopping bag. "I've got a litter box in here. Her mother has already trained her, just make sure you show her where the box is so she doesn't get confused."

"How old is she?"

"Six weeks. Here's her bowl and a week's supply of food. Don't make the mistake of feeding her milk. It might make her sick."

"Lacey, this is so nice of you, but—"

Lacey stood up and crumpled the empty shopping bag in her hands. "I promised Erin I would do this."

Ah.

"The kitten is for Shelley."

CHAPTER 18

That night the kitten slept on a blanket that I placed in the middle of the bed between myself and Shelley. When Shelley woke up, the kitten was stretching, front paws out, rear end tucked high. Shelley was instantly entranced. "What's her name?"

"She's yours, Shelley. Your mom asked Lacey to give her to you. You can name her whatever you want."

"Really?" Shelley giggled as the kitten walked clumsily off the blanket and tumbled into the down comforter. Gently the little girl scooped up the kitten and placed her on her chest.

The kitten mewed and tried to lick Shelley's finger.

"I think she's hungry. We should also take her to the bathroom." I rolled out of bed to show Shelley where we were keeping the kitty litter and the food and water bowls.

After the kitten had done her business and taken a few munches of her food, Shelley asked, "Can I show the twins?"

It was Saturday and Devin and Jamie were still sleeping. They might not be thrilled about being woken before nine o'clock, but I figured a new kitten would be worth it.

"Sure. Go ahead."

As I dressed, I wondered how Murphy would react if we took the kitten with us when we went for breakfast. I couldn't leave the little thing alone in the house. Another option would be to have breakfast at home this morning, but it seemed important to keep the same routine as much as we could.

Besides, I was afraid that if I didn't see Murphy as soon as possible, things would become awkward between us.

I stared at my reflection as I brushed my hair and considered the question I'd been too tired to consider last night. *What was I going to tell Burke?*

I'd called him when I'd gotten home to assure him I was fine, but we hadn't talked for long. Now I wondered just how much I was obliged to tell him.

We'd been dating for almost two months. We'd slept together on a couple of occasions. Did that constitute a serious relationship? Should I be feeling guilty about what had happened between Murphy and me? What were the rules to dating in the twenty-first century? I wished Erin was here for me to ask.

More quickly than I'd guessed, life returned to a steady routine in our house. Shelley started back at school. The kitten adjusted to our home as if she'd always lived here. The twins resumed their active social lives, accommodating without apparent difficulty the addition of a little sister and a pet to the family.

Yet, while the wheels of domestication rolled smoothly through the last days of November, there was a dark hole in the center of our lives that we all stepped gingerly around.

It wasn't that we never spoke of Erin. For Shelley's sake, I knew it was important to talk as much as possible about how we were feeling and how much Erin was missed.

But stories and memories would never be enough to fill the void that Erin had left. And I knew I wasn't the only one who felt a pain that words couldn't express. At night Shelley would wake up from nightmares, crying for her mom. Even Devin and Jamie— self-centered teenagers that they were—indulged in the sniffles now and then.

As for Murphy, he held his grief in so tightly, no one could guess how bad he felt. To my surprise, he allowed the kitten in his diner as long as we kept her in a carry case he'd bought for that purpose.

Burke continued to call me several times a week, and we went out at least once a week on top of that. I'd decided not to tell him about Murphy. As Murphy himself had said, it was just one of those things. No sense dwelling on what had happened or giving it an importance it didn't deserve.

Work was hectic as I struggled to catch up with weeks of neglected background checks, administrative details and casework. I stopped declining clients and started accepting work again.

I'd been worried that without Erin, I'd be over my head with the P.I. business. But I was better equipped than I'd thought I was, and Erin's contacts, including two colleagues from an agency called Backtrack Investigations, were a tremendous help.

A few weeks after Erin's memorial service, I set up a meeting with Ava. I'd been cleaning Adam's condo on schedule, but hadn't prepared a report for Ava in over a month. I'd told her I didn't have time, with Erin being sick and all.

But I could no longer postpone what had to be said.

Ava was waiting at the counter when I arrived and I slid onto the stool next to her.

"Hi, Lauren. I'm sorry about Erin."

"Thanks. It's been tough. Especially for her daughter. But, we're trying to get back to normal and that includes work."

Ava touched my arm anxiously. "Have you been to Adam's recently? Is he still seeing that girl?"

I didn't answer at first. I waited for Murphy to fill my mug, then I added cream and gave it a stir. I noticed Ava was looking for the briefcase I usually carried.

"Where's your report?" Ava's patience was clearly slipping. "You did clean his condo yesterday, didn't you?"

"Yes." I'd left it impeccably clean, having finally caught up on all the outstanding problems, including the blinds.

"So…?"

"Ava, I left a note at Adam's explaining that I wouldn't be cleaning for him anymore."

"What?"

"I can't keep doing this. I don't think you should, either."

"But I need to know, Lauren. Is he still seeing that Mallory girl? Are they getting serious?"

I didn't know how to tell her what I'd figured out that week. I'd hoped that her interest might have finally waned and I wouldn't need to.

But obviously, that wasn't the case.

"Ava, there's something about Adam you don't understand. He isn't the right man for you."

"How can you say that? He's perfect. I wouldn't have devoted all this time and energy to winning him over if I wasn't sure of that."

"But Ava." I filled my lungs with air. "You know how I haven't noticed any girlie things in the condo? Just the extra toothbrush?"

She nodded. "That means they aren't very serious. It's just a casual thing."

"It could have meant that. Only…when I checked out the medicine cabinet this week, I noticed something that didn't register before."

She looked at me blankly.

"There were two razors in the cabinet, Ava. Two *men's* razors."

Ava stared at me in stunned surprise. "Are you saying… Is Adam *gay?*"

"I think so." When I'd become suspicious myself, I'd gone back onto his computer and taken another look at the porn. "I'm positive, actually."

I'd also checked a different in-box file labeled Jake and had found e-mail correspondence going back several months. The mysterious J. Mallory uncovered.

Ava let her head sink into her arms on the counter. "Oh, God, why didn't I guess? Now I've wasted all this time. Next month I'm going to be *twenty-five*."

"Trust me, Ava. You'll have many opportunities to find someone. It's going to be okay."

When she finally pulled herself together and tried to pay me, I refused the money. As she left, I said, "Ava? If you decide to snoop into the life of your next prospect...don't call me, okay?"

She grinned feebly, then left.

With perfect timing, Murphy came by with a refill. "Never turn away a paying client, Lauren."

"Interesting philosophy, Murphy. Is that why you're always so sweet to *your* customers?"

His eyes narrowed. "You're starting to be as much of a smart-ass as Erin was."

"What can I say? I learned from the best."

"Yeah. She was a pain all right. Such a pain, I can't believe I miss having her around." The grief in his eyes belied the casualness of his words.

"It's hard, isn't it? I hate having to see her side of

our house every day, all silent and dark. I just can't get over the feeling that she's in there, hiding, playing a prank on us all."

"Speaking of that house... Have you decided what you're going to do with it?"

"Not really. The four of us are pretty cramped—we need at least another bedroom. I suppose it makes the most sense to sell my side and Erin's, then move into something bigger. But uprooting the kids at this point doesn't seem like a great idea."

"Have you considered renovating the house into one home?"

"Do you think that's feasible?"

"Sure. You'd have a center-staircase plan with a big kitchen at the back and six bedrooms."

"Wouldn't that be a dream?" I let myself consider the possibility. "I could combine the two back rooms into a big office for Creative Investigations and there'd still be enough space for the girls to have their own bedrooms."

"The extra bathroom would come in handy, too."

"Would it ever. Maybe I should have a contractor come in and give me a quote."

"I have a buddy who would give you a deal. Want his number?"

"Sure. Burke just had his roof replaced, too. I should see if he would recommend that outfit as well."

"Burke. So you're still dating the doctor?"

"Yes. In fact we have plans for tonight."

There'd been some warmth in Murphy's eyes just minutes ago. I could have sworn there had been. But now what I saw in his deep brown eyes made me cold to my bones.

I realized I hadn't mentioned Burke since the memorial service. "Murphy, you knew, right? I never said—"

"Forget it, Lauren. Just forget I said anything."

He headed back to the kitchen and I let my eyes follow him. Even though he'd tried to deny it, Murphy had reacted like a jealous lover. But he'd never shown any special interest in me since our night together. He certainly hadn't asked me out.

So what was his problem?

The girls had received another postcard from their father that day. They'd left it on the kitchen table and once dinner was over and the dishes were cleared away, I flipped the card over.

Gary was still in Chennai. He'd discovered a new favorite food: *uppumas*, some sort of semolina mash.

The highest good here is to feed the poor. Can you imagine what Toronto would be like if all our neighbors had an attitude like that?

Oh, really. I tossed the card back on the table. The question Gary should be asking himself was *How many poor do you need to feed before you can convince yourself you're a good person, even though you deserted your wife and daughters?*

For someone seeking self-awareness, Gary was an incredibly slow learner. His smug superiority was certainly wearing thin on me.

Yet, between the lines, I thought Gary sounded less satisfied than usual with his pursuit of spiritual fulfillment. For the first time, he'd asked questions about the girls—and me. Plus, he'd included a forwarding address and asked the girls to write to him.

Whether they would or not would be up to them. But I couldn't help suspect that this reaching out might be the real beginning of Gary's search for self-awareness.

From the day he'd left me, I'd wondered where we had gone wrong—where *I* had gone wrong. Now, for the first time, I wondered if we had.

Maybe the divorce had been the right thing. Not just for him, but for me, too.

Had I really been happy with Gary? When he'd left, had I missed Gary, the person, or just Gary, the husband?

There was a distinction between the two, I saw now.

When you missed someone you loved, you thought about the way they smiled. You imagined telling them something that happened to you that day and what they would have thought about it.

I'd been miserable and depressed after Gary had left me. But I hadn't really missed him. Not the way I missed Erin.

Now what did that say about my marriage?

Before my date with Burke, I made dinner for the girls. Shelley wasn't eating much lately, so to tempt her appetite I made the lentil curry that was one of her favorites. As I stirred spices into the sautéing onions, Shelley ran around the kitchen trailing a piece of string for Honey.

That was what Shelley had elected to call her pet in the end. Given the cat's golden coloring and sweet disposition, it seemed an excellent choice to me.

"Look, Lauren! Isn't she funny?"

The kitten was chasing her tail now. She really was

the most amusing thing. Erin would have thought it was a hoot.

She was so right to have insisted we adopt a kitten. It was the perfect distraction for Shelley. Not that Shelley wasn't still missing her mother. But Honey helped. She helped us all.

By the time Devin and Jamie arrived home from school, I had the meal ready. I was disappointed that it didn't taste the same, even though I'd followed the recipe precisely. Though the kids didn't complain, I noticed none of them ate very much.

"Maybe I shouldn't go out with Burke tonight. Would you guys like to watch a movie together?"

"Mom, don't be crazy," Jamie said. "Shelley will be asleep in a couple of hours and I don't know about Devin, but I've got tons of homework. Go out and have fun."

Devin agreed. "You keep canceling your plans with him. He's going to start to think that you don't like him."

Jamie helped herself to another slice of bread. "You *do* like him, don't you, Mom?"

"Of course I do." What woman wouldn't like Burke? He was nice company, attractive and utterly dependable. He really enjoyed the girls, too. The couple of times he'd dropped by the house for a family meal, I hadn't sensed the slightest ripple of discord. He'd already told me he enjoyed hanging out at our place. Apparently he enjoyed noise and mayhem.

I guessed it must be lonely living alone. At least I didn't have to do that.

"Then go out with him, Mom. You aren't getting any younger."

"Gee, thanks, Jamie."

When the girls offered to clean up the dishes, I went upstairs to change. I found myself remembering the second time I'd gone out with Burke. Erin had offered all sorts of advice.

Now as I picked through various possibilities in my closet, I could imagine what Erin would say.

That sweater set is so boring. Why don't you just take along a pair of knitting needles and a ball of yarn.... No, don't wear the trousers—pick a skirt. Flat shoes, again? Don't you own any heels?

Then, when it came for the final touch of makeup and selection of jewelry... *Ditch the pearls, Lauren. I have just the funky necklace to go with that....*

I checked the clasp on my pearls, then sank to the bed.

Much as I knew it would be good for me to get out,

I didn't feel up to it. All I wanted was to change into my jammies, snuggle next to the girls and maybe watch a movie or something.

But Jamie was right. I'd already turned down two of Burke's invitations. If I didn't go this time, he was going to think I didn't like him.

And I did like him. He was the only sane thing in my life right now.

Downstairs the doorbell rang and I heard someone dash to open the door. It was probably Shelley, anxious to show Burke her kitten's latest trick.

I forced myself to stand. Slowly I made my way down the stairs. I knew why I felt so reluctant. I was depressed, that was all. And the best way to beat depression was to push yourself to get out and do the things that you knew you would enjoy once you felt better again.

"Hello, Burke."

He turned to look at me. Honey was curled in his hand, sleeping. "You look lovely, Lauren."

"Thank you." There was no need to give anyone instructions. The girls knew better than me how to give Shelley her bath and put her to sleep. They also had Burke's cell-phone number and knew exactly under which circumstances to use it.

Our evening passed so pleasantly, I wondered why I'd been hesitant to go in the first place. I appreciated Burke's efforts to keep to lighter topics; however, on the way home, his mood grew more serious.

"I think your girls are great, Lauren. And you know I absolutely approve of your decision to become Shelley's guardian."

"I'm glad." I sensed this was leading somewhere.

"It's just that, with all the kids around, it's hard for us to be together."

I digested the comment. "You mean there's no opportunity for us to sleep together?"

He laughed. "Yeah, that too. I'd like some input from you on the best way to deal with this. Do you think we could get away for an evening once a month? Go to Niagara-on-the-Lake, or maybe up north to the Muskoka Sands?"

Again, because of my depression, I couldn't summon very much enthusiasm for the idea. But I could understand Burke's position. On the whole, he was being very accommodating. "That sounds nice to me."

Burke smiled. "Could you get away next week?"

"That might be a little soon to arrange. How about the following weekend?"

"Terrific. I'll book us a room for the Saturday night."

He reached over to take my hand and, as he entwined his fingers with mine, I felt a resurgence of my guilt about the time with Murphy. Maybe I should make a confession and get this off my chest. Burke was such an understanding guy. Surely he'd handle it okay.

But it wasn't fear of Burke's reaction that kept me from speaking. It was something else, something I couldn't explain even to myself. I just didn't want to tell him.

During breakfast at the diner the next morning, the girls teased me about my date.

"So what time did you get home, Mom?" Devin asked.

"Umm…midnight?"

Jamie laughed. "We're going to have set you a curfew, young lady."

I shook my head. It was great that the girls took my dating in stride this way. At least I thought it was.

"I've got only one order of blueberry pancakes with whipped cream," Murphy said, coming up on my left side. "Jamie, do you want them?"

"Me, me!" Shelley bounced on her seat.

"What was that? Devin, is this your order?"

Shelley giggled. "No, Murphy, Devin likes fruit salad. *I* want the pancakes."

"Oh, that's right. Why do I always forget that?" Murphy set the plate in front of the little girl, then leaned over to say hi to Honey. The kitten was inside her padded carrying case, sitting on the counter right by Shelley's plate.

"How's the tiger?" Murphy asked.

Shelley giggled again. "Honey is a *cat*."

"I'm not so sure. Did you see those claws? I think she's going to grow up to be a tiger. Or at least a bobcat."

He went back for the twins' plates. "How's Bio ten going, Devin?"

"Don't remind me. I hate science," she groaned.

"Not as much as I hate math," her sister countered. Jamie dug her fork into her pale, no-yolk scrambled eggs.

"You guys remember my offer," Murphy said, before disappearing into the kitchen.

"What was Murphy talking about?" I tapped my empty mug on the counter, trying not to feel ignored. In the past, Murphy had always poured my coffee first thing. We'd been here fifteen minutes and I hadn't had so much as a drop so far.

"He offered to tutor us," Devin said. "He helps some of the other customers, too, when they decide to go back to school."

"Murphy is a tutor?"

"He says math and science are his specialties."

"They are?"

For the third time, Murphy came up from behind me. He set down a plate. "And finally, one house breakfast."

I wrinkled my nose. The eggs were overdone, the hash browns were soggy and the bacon looked cold. I lifted my mug. "Could I have a—"

But Murphy was gone.

"Great." I looked at my plate again wondering how I was going to eat any of this without coffee to wash it down.

At least the three girls seemed happy. Even Shelley was eating her breakfast with gusto.

I twisted around. Murphy was behind the cash register, making change for one of his customers. I thought he'd been looking at me, too, but he glanced away so quickly I couldn't be sure.

I sighed with exasperation. What was up with that man? Lately, he'd been driving me crazy.

CHAPTER 19

Two more weeks passed and then it was time for our getaway to Niagara-on-the-Lake. Burke picked me up mid-afternoon on Saturday for the two-hour drive.

Gazing out the side window of Burke's car at the hibernating vineyards, I thought about the many times I had taken this trip with my parents when I was a little girl.

"I haven't driven this way in more than a year," Burke said.

"Was that with your wife?"

He nodded. "Stephanie loved the Shaw Festival."

"So did—does—my mother. When I was a girl, my parents would take me every year." With Christmas coming I really should do something about healing the rift with my mother. But it wouldn't be easy, especially now that I'd taken Shelley into the family. When I'd made the call to inform them, my mother had taken it as another sign I was losing my marbles.

"Where did you stay?" Burke asked. "When you came up here with your parents?"

"The Prince of Wales Hotel."

He laughed.

"You and Stephanie, too?"

"Yes. And I hope you don't mind, but that's where I booked our reservation as well."

Did I mind going to the same hotel where he'd once taken his wife? I decided I didn't. "It'll be fun. The old hotel is kind of an institution in that town. It would be strange to stay anywhere else."

Burke smiled warmly. "You have no idea how much I've been looking forward to this."

"Me, too." Though I really hadn't had the time or mental energy to spend on anticipation, now that I was in Burke's car, headed toward our destination, I did feel more lighthearted than I'd been since I'd found out about Erin's diagnosis. "I only wish it wasn't off-season and we could take in a play."

"We'll go again in July," Burke promised. "Maybe we could take the girls, just like your parents used to do with you."

I felt a welling of tenderness toward him. "I love that you're so accepting of my family."

"I've always liked kids and yours are great. I try to avoid useless regrets, but it's hard not to wish that Stephanie could have had children. It would have made such a difference to me this year."

"Children give you a reason to go on. They *force* you to go on."

"I could have used some of that."

And the really sad thing was that Burke would have made a terrific father. Sometimes you make the best decisions you can at the time and life still doesn't work out the way you planned.

Burke slowed the car as we approached the town limits. Lake Ontario was to our left, the pretty town of Niagara-on-the-Lake to our right.

We had arrived.

"Breakfast is served," Burke announced.

I stretched luxuriously in the cloud of bed linens. I couldn't believe it was morning already. I hadn't slept through the night since... I couldn't remember the last time.

Burke set a tray on the bed between us, then

propped his pillows against the headboard and crawled back under the covers.

"Coffee, my sweet?"

"Mm. Absolutely." I inched my way into a sitting position, too, then brushed my hair off my forehead. The tray was laden with two silver-covered plates, coffee and accoutrements, and a bowl of ruby-red strawberries. "When did you order all this?"

"When I booked the room." He handed me a cup of coffee. "Be careful."

I took a sip. It was lovely, if a little on the weak side. "You're spoiling me."

Every detail about our little getaway had been perfect. From the flowers Burke had ordered delivered to our room, to the chocolate soufflé at the end of our four-course dinner...

To the lovemaking last night.

"I thought we could walk around downtown for a few hours before we head back to the city," Burke said.

"Or we could spend another hour in our room... Checkout isn't until eleven."

"That, too, of course. I won't pretend it wasn't the first thing on my mind this morning. But I thought I'd feed you first."

"You're so thoughtful."

"Even though I have ulterior motives?" He selected a strawberry, held it out for me to take a nibble, then slid the remainder into his mouth.

"Even though."

I drank my coffee, ate most of my omelet, then went to the washroom to brush my teeth. When I returned, Burke had cleared the bed of all signs of our breakfast.

"Come here," he said, holding open his arms.

I got back into bed and he pulled me up on top of him. He was already hard and just that knowledge brought on a rush of heat and wetness. As he ran his hands down the sides of my head, to my shoulders, then down my back, I hitched up the silky slip I'd worn to bed and straddled his hips.

"Lauren. You're so lovely. I love you so much."

We strained to kiss and I felt him gliding inside of me. I rotated my hips, heard him moan in response.

Slowly I found my rhythm. Closed my eyes. As I tipped back my head, he slid his hands up from my belly to cup my breasts. The moment his fingers made contact with my nipples, I felt the first contractions begin.

My orgasm was slow and every bit as luxurious as the hotel bed we were lying on. I sensed Burke coming with me, and when I toppled to my side, spent, he reached out to hug me.

"That was even more delicious than breakfast," I said. I couldn't remember enjoying sex this much when I'd been married. Or maybe I had in the beginning.

"Lauren, you make me so happy. I know this is soon. Probably too soon, but I have to ask anyway. Will you marry me?"

What? I sat up and stared at him as my mind struggled to process what he'd just said.

"Relax, Lauren. Come here—let me hold you again."

Reluctantly I let him draw me back into his arms. I wondered if he could feel the rapid, panicked drumming of my heart.

"I'm sorry. Bad timing, huh?"

"I—I'm flattered, Burke. Really, I am. I just never expected—"

"I know. It was too soon. It's just that I'm so happy when I'm with you."

"I'm glad."

"You have no idea how much I hate going home to that empty house at the end of each day. Your place is so warm and busy and full of activity."

"Well, it's definitely full of activity."

He squeezed me tightly. "You're luckier than you know."

I hadn't thought of myself that way, as lucky, for a long time. And yet he was right. I was very, very fortunate.

And now, suddenly, I had something else wonderful to feel lucky about. A marriage proposal from a really terrific man. I liked him, my girls liked him, and I had no doubt that my parents would totally approve, too.

"I know my place isn't big enough," Burke said. "I thought we would buy something new, something close to the girls' school."

Goodbye Carbon Road. Goodbye crowded subways and garbage on the streets and terrible BLT sandwiches at Murphy's Grill. Goodbye and good riddance.

"I don't mean to pressure you," Burke added. "I feel one hundred percent certain that this is the right thing to do. But I respect your need for a little more time."

"It's just that I'm still dealing with losing Erin. And so is Shelley. Do you think you could wait until after Christmas for an answer?"

"Two more weeks?"

"The time will go quickly. December always does.

And it'll give Shelley time to adjust to life without her mother."

"I guess that's fair. I promise I'll wait until December twenty-sixth before I bring up the subject again."

The first week after Burke's proposal did pass quickly. I barely thought of Christmas as I focused on assimilating Shelley into the family and getting on top of the work at the agency. Burke spent several of his evenings with us, but he didn't push for time alone with me again.

He seemed happy to help me cook dinner, then sit around watching television or reading in the evening. Sometimes, when I had paperwork to catch up on, he would putter around the old house, installing a new light fixture here, doing a little caulking there.

On the fifteenth of December, I went into Murphy's diner around noon, after snagging the photos I needed for an insurance fraud case I'd been working on all week.

I sank onto one of the stools, my body already anticipating the hit from one of Murphy's cups of coffee. My hand even trembled a little as I reached out for the mug he'd filled.

"You look beat."

Trust Murphy to hit me with a compliment first thing. "Maybe. But I got the evidence I need so I don't care."

"Is that why you haven't been in the past few days? Work?"

I nodded. "Sometimes when I've been working late the twins take pity on me and let me sleep in." I gulped more coffee down. "I haven't had any time to start preparing for Christmas."

Murphy looked at me like I was crazy. "What's to prepare? You buy a tree, you buy a turkey. Done."

"I wish it could be that easy." I felt a lot of pressure about this Christmas. It would be the twins' second one without their father. And Shelley's first without her mother. "Do you know if Erin had any special traditions that she would have liked me to carry on?"

Again, Murphy looked at me like I was nuts. "You're definitely making this into too big a deal." He crashed some cups into a plastic tub, then stalked off to the kitchen.

"Whoa. I guess I touched a nerve there."

I spoke more to myself than anyone else and was surprised when Stan stirred from his seat near the back and came to sit next to me.

"Yes, you did touch a nerve. But you had no way of knowing, so I wouldn't feel badly."

"I don't." I took another sip of coffee and knew it was a lie. I did feel bad. I just didn't want to admit it. "Frankly I'm not surprised to find out Murphy is a grinch."

Stan said nothing, and yet I knew he had more to say on the subject. Finally I caved and asked, "Why is Murphy so set against Christmas?"

When Stan still didn't say anything, my imagination offered a possibility. "Does the reason have anything to do with his sister and her children?"

Stan seemed sink a little into his stool. "The fire happened Christmas eve."

"Oh, no."

"The whole family was sleeping, except Murphy. He and his father had had a fight, and he'd gone out to find his buddies. Apparently his father kept drinking, then around one in the morning set torch to the place and ran."

The stark explanation was just too much.

"I can't believe that. Or what I mean to say is I don't want to believe it." How could any father deliberately destroy his family? His wife, his daughter, his grandchildren…and on Christmas eve, no less?

"He was a bitter old man. Unhappy with his life, unhappy with himself. Nothing was ever his fault, you understand. He always had to have someone to blame."

"Poor Murphy."

"Yeah, but he found a soul mate in Erin. She had her reasons to dislike Christmas, too."

"I'm not sure I'm up to hearing another story like the last one, Stan."

"I know it isn't easy to hear this stuff, but it'll help you understand. See, Erin was kicked out of her home on Christmas Day."

"I thought she ran away?"

"That's not quite how it went. She'd finally gathered her courage to tell her mother what was going on with the stepdad. She wanted her mom to kick the loser out and start over without him. Instead, her mother kicked her out."

"I can't imagine doing that to my kid."

"So now you know why the holidays weren't too popular around here. Erin and Murphy liked to celebrate what they called an un-Christmas Christmas."

"What was that like?"

"They'd hide presents around the diner for Shelley. Sort of like Easter, you know? Then Murphy would make burgers and milkshakes. He'd open the doors and people would come in and he'd feed them for free."

"Feed them burgers and milkshakes? On Christmas?"

"Yeah. He keeps it pretty low-key, but word gets around on the street. He always has a good crowd."

"But Murphy makes terrible burgers."

"Correction. Murphy's *cook* makes terrible burgers. His aren't too bad."

"If Murphy's so good in the kitchen, why doesn't he work there all the time?"

"Are you kidding? You know Murphy's a people person."

I snorted, spewing coffee onto the counter. Stan passed me a wad of napkins.

"He's still hiding out in the kitchen," Stan commented.

"I must have really ticked him off mentioning the C word."

"He'll get over himself," Stan predicted.

"I hope so. I'm going to have to find a way to combine the un-Christmas that Shelley is used to, with the real Christmas that my girls have always had."

"How are you going to get Murphy to buy into that?"

I eyed the door to the kitchen. The door that

refused to budge, no matter how hard I willed it to. Murphy was definitely annoyed. But I wasn't too worried. Murphy had his soft spots. And Shelley was definitely number one on the list.

In the end, Christmas came off surprisingly smoothly. The girls and I put up a small tree and cooked a turkey meal with trimmings on Christmas eve. I called my parents to invite them. They declined, but countered with an offer of New Year's dinner at their place. I accepted.

The process of reconciliation was finally in place.

Burke came over for the Christmas eve dinner. He read *The Night Before Christmas* to Shelley, then insisted everyone watch *Miracle on 34th Street* together.

In the morning my girls and I went for our traditional breakfast at Murphy's. The place was closed. We were the only customers. Shelley squealed as she ran around the diner, searching out Murphy's gifts in all the old hiding places.

Everyone chipped in and helped when it came time to serve the burgers and the milkshakes. Many of the men and women and children who came in were obviously needy. I felt as if I'd never spent my Christmas in a more meaningful way.

It was past Shelley's bedtime when we finally closed shop. Murphy walked home with us, carrying Shelley in his arms. I ran ahead to unlock the front door.

"That was a cool Christmas, Murph," Jamie said as she kicked off her shoes, then ran upstairs.

"I liked it, too," Devin agreed, before following her sister.

Murphy caught my gaze. "Where should I take this one?" he asked, indicating the sleeping child in his arms.

"She's with Devin this week." The girls alternated having Shelley in their rooms. It was a short-term solution and I knew I had to make a decision about our living arrangements soon. But there was no sense going ahead with the renovation if I was going to marry Burke.

Only I still didn't know if I was, or not.

I'd thought about our future a lot the past few days. If I accepted Burke's proposal, I'd have my old life back. And so would the twins. As for Shelley, she'd have a quality of life Erin could only have dreamed of providing for her. Living with Burke, there'd be no question of affording private schooling for all the girls, including university.

And the girls would have a father again. It didn't matter so much to Jamie and Devin. They'd grown up with a dad, and they'd have one again once he got tired of India and realized that he kind of missed golfing and roast-beef dinners and TV.

But Shelley had never had a father and she was young enough that she and Burke would have a chance to really bond.

What more could Erin have wanted for her daughter?

When I thought about it that way, I felt like I almost *owed* it to Erin and Shelley to accept the proposal.

Murphy came back down the stairs. "She's still asleep," he said. "Didn't even bat an eyelash."

"She's had a long day." I hesitated. Murphy had been in one of his better moods today. A few times in the kitchen we'd shared a laugh. And once, when we'd both gone to the freezer in the same moment, I'd thought I'd seen something in his eyes that reminded me of the time we'd slept together.

Not that I necessarily wanted to be reminded of that. Still, for Shelley's sake it was important that we remain friends.

"Would you like a drink? I could open a bottle of wine."

Murphy's eyes were dark as he focused them on me.

I felt shivers at the nape of my neck when he said, "That sounds nice."

But I'd no sooner turned for the kitchen than I heard a vehicle out on the street. Ten seconds later, there was a knock at my front door.

I hesitated before answering it, glancing back at Murphy to gauge his reaction.

"Is that Burke?" he asked, his mouth and jaw held tightly under control.

"Probably. I wasn't expecting him, but I can't think who else it would be."

"Do you get a kick out of torturing me, Lauren?"

"What?"

Before I could say anything more, he brushed past me to open the door. Burke looked at him, startled, then Murphy pushed past him, too.

I didn't try to call Murphy back. I had no idea what to say to him, I was still reeling from his remark. In the past month, Murphy had made his feelings for me abundantly clear…he didn't have any.

But what if I had misread him?

"I'm sorry, I guess I should have called," Burke said. "Obviously I interrupted something."

I'd told Burke all about our plans for Christmas Day, just as he'd explained that he wanted to spend the day with his folks. "Murphy carried Shelley home for me. She fell asleep about an hour ago, curled up in an armchair in the back of the kitchen."

"Oh."

Realizing Burke was still standing in the foyer, I closed the door and locked it. "A glass of wine?"

"Sure." He followed me to the kitchen. I could feel the energy radiating off him as he watched me open the bottle and pour two glasses.

"I hope you don't mind me coming by so late. I just had to see you."

I did mind—but I didn't have the heart to say so. All I wanted now was to crawl into bed…and ponder Murphy's parting remark. Instead, Burke and I took our drinks to the living room.

"How was your day with your parents?"

"It was great. We started with brunch at the…"

Several times during his answer, I had to stifle a yawn. Finally Burke noticed.

"You're exhausted."

"Shelley woke up just after six. It's been a long day." I started to rise from the sofa, expecting that I'd given him his cue to leave. But he stopped me with a hand on my arm.

"Give me five minutes more, Lauren."

Again I could sense a contained excitement about him. What did he have to tell me?

"It's four minutes to midnight," he said.

"Yes, it's very late."

"Four minutes to December twenty-sixth," he elaborated.

And finally my tired, fuzzy brain realized that he was hoping for an answer to his proposal.

"In three and a half more minutes, Christmas will be over. You don't know how difficult it's been to keep my promise. I can't wait an extra minute, Lauren. Will you marry me?"

In my mind I had decided to say yes. Burke was so attentive and kind. He'd be a great companion and a tremendous father as well. Though money wasn't the most important thing, I had to admit it would be a relief not to worry about it and to be able to afford a nice home in a good neighborhood again.

The marriage made sense from all angles. Burke seemed to love my girls almost as much as he loved me. What more could I want?

And yet I couldn't get Murphy's words out of my head. Or the way I'd felt after he'd said them—that zap of crazy, illogical anticipation.

But anticipation for what?

Did I think Murphy was in love with me?

Was I in love with him?

But that was crazy. *In love.* What did *in love* mean to a woman of forty-five with three daughters and a kitten to worry about? I couldn't see myself married to Murphy, whereas it was very easy to picture myself married to Burke.

Burke took my hand. He leaned forward to press a kiss on my cheek, then the side of my neck. Nuzzling my ear, he whispered, "Say yes, Lauren. Let me take care of you and the girls. Let us be a family. A *real* family."

Oh my Lord, I didn't know what to say. If only Erin were here. What would she advise?

I closed my eyes, tried to conjure my friend's voice inside my head.

But Erin was silent. I heard nothing at all.

"Burke, you know how I feel about you. I'm very tempted to say yes..."

He kissed me gently on the mouth. "Then do it, Lauren."

"But I'm so tired I can hardly put a sentence together. Please let me give you my answer tomorrow. I want to be sure, Burke. And I want to be fully conscious."

He made a sound, a combination groan and laugh. "I knew I should have called first."

"I'm sorry. It's just that I wasn't expecting to talk to you about this until tomorrow. And yes, I know that *officially* it's Boxing Day right now, but to my body and my mind it's definitely still Christmas."

"Okay. I get it. We'll make it tomorrow. Lunch or dinner?"

"Whatever you want."

"Then lunch. Twelve o'clock?"

"Thank you for being so understanding about this."

"I wouldn't be if I didn't know that we are going to be perfect together."

My heart dipped a little at that. Where did his certainty come from? I wished I could have a little of it for myself.

As I let him out the door, my doubts grew heavier. I had a failed marriage behind me...and I didn't even understand why it had failed. So how could I be sure that this one would fare any better?

I didn't want to end up with two ex-husbands on my résumé.

But at the same time, the lure of security and comfort and belonging were pulling hard. I kept reminding myself that I wasn't making this decision for just myself. I had to think of Devin, and Jamie, and Shelley, as well.

I went upstairs to bed where I slept fitfully until a dream startled me into wakefulness. I rolled over to read the digits on my bedside alarm and sighed. Six in the morning.

I tried closing my eyes, hoping to drift back into unconsciousness. But no luck.

Might as well give in and get up. I dressed in jeans and a T-shirt, then crept to the kitchen where I poured a glass of juice. It was still an hour before Shelley's usual time to get out of bed. But the little girl had been so exhausted last night she'd probably sleep in beyond that.

For sure the twins would.

Unaccustomed to being alone in a silent house, I went to sit in the living room by the front window. The kitten found me there and curled into my lap.

"Hello, little Honey." I tickled under her chin. "Do you know what I should do about Burke?"

The kitten purred, then rolled onto her back.

"What kind of answer is that?"

I scratched all the kitten's favorite parts, then set her on the floor. Honey batted my toe for a minute, then wandered to her carrier by the door. She climbed in, curled herself into a ball, then looked at me expectantly.

"What are you telling me, Honey?" Did she think it was time to go for breakfast? But the girls were still sleeping and the diner didn't open until seven.

On the other hand, Murphy was usually there by six. Maybe he'd let me in early.

I slipped on a jacket and walked through two inches of fresh snow with Honey's carrier strapped on my shoulder. Our white Christmas had arrived a day too late, but it was still pretty. Even Dupont Street looked quaint with a dusting of powder to soften its hard edges.

At the diner I pressed my face to the glass door and peered inside. Murphy had his back to me, setting up the coffee machines. I tapped on the glass.

He turned, then seemed to freeze. Had he recognized me? Was he going to let me in, or what?

Finally he crossed the room and undid the locks.

"It's a bad sign when you start needing it this early," he said.

"I assume you're talking about coffee?"

"What else?" He took the kitten's carrier from me and set it on the usual place at the counter. Without another word he got a fresh mug and filled it. Then he passed me a muffin.

"Sorry, it's day-old. The kitchen isn't open yet."

I didn't care. I sat there eating and drinking and realized why I couldn't make myself accept Burke's proposal.

I liked coming here for breakfast. It was the highlight of my day and I didn't want to give it up.

What did that say about me and my life, that coffee and a greasy egg breakfast meant that much to me?

And yet they did.

"Burke asked me to marry him. I'm going to say no."

Murphy dropped the pan he'd been carrying. "What did you say?"

"I think you heard me."

He came around the counter at the same time that I stood up. We stared at one another for a long time.

"I don't want to get married, Lauren."

Until that moment I hadn't realized that I didn't, either. "Neither do I."

"And I don't want you to leave."

I stepped forward and he opened his arms to embrace me.

He smelled like coffee and French fries and grilled meat. I kissed him the way I breathed air—because I had to.

He ran his hands up my arms, my shoulders, then gently curved his fingers around my neck.

I tugged at him to come closer. Closer. Closer. I angled my head for a deeper kiss.

And that was when I heard the quiet snap. Then the pearls from my necklace began to fall to the old wooden floor. I glanced down in time to see one of them disappear between the gap of two boards.

Murphy's laugh was low. "I didn't mean to do that. Honest."

"It doesn't matter." I would retrieve the pearls later. Now all I wanted was to kiss him again.

But this time a part of my mind hung back. I thought about the day I'd moved into this neighborhood—a middle-aged woman in cashmere and pearls. Back then I'd felt as if I'd lost my place in the world and would never reclaim it.

That woman felt like a stranger now. A year and a half after my husband had left me, I'd finally found my better half.

And the man in my arms, and the street beyond us both, and the house on Carbon Road with three sleeping girls...these were the things that felt like my home.

True Confessions
of the
Stratford Park PTA

by **Nancy Robards Thompson**

The journey of four women through midlife;
man trouble; and their children's middle
school hormones—as they find their place
in this world...

Available October 2006
TheNextNovel.com

HN62

A stunning novel of love and renewal…

Everyone knows sisters like the Sams girls—
three women trying their best to be good
daughters, mothers and wives. Then in one
cataclysmic moment everything changes…
and the sisters have to uncover every shrouded
secret and risk lifetime bonds to ensure the
survival of all they love.

Graceland

by Lynne Hugo

Available October 2006
TheNextNovel.com

HARLEQUIN®
Next™

There's got to be a mourning-after!

Saturday, September 22

1) Get a ~~dog~~ cat
2) Get a man
3) Get adventurous (go skinny-dipping)
4) Get a LIFE!

Jill Townsend is learning to step beyond the safe world she's always known to take the leap into Merry Widowhood.

The Merry Widow's Diary

by Susan Crosby

Just like a blue moon, friendship is a beautiful thing

Hoping to rekindle a sense of purpose, Lola resurrects a childhood dream and buys a blue beach house. When she drags three of her fun-loving, margarita-sipping friends out for some gossip and good times, they discover the missing spark in their relationships.

Once in a Blue Moon

by Lenora Worth

Available October 2006
TheNextNovel.com

HN64

REQUEST YOUR FREE BOOKS!

2 FREE NOVELS TO INTRODUCE YOU TO OUR BRAND-NEW LINE!

There's the life you planned. And there's what comes next.